DO NOT DISTURB

DO NOT DISTURB

HOTEL SEX STORIES

EDITED BY
RACHEL KRAMER BUSSEL

CLEIS
PRESS

Published in the United States.
Cleis Press Inc., P.O. Box 14697, San Francisco, California 94114

Printed in the United States.
Cover design: Scott Idleman
Cover photograph: FEV Create Inc.
Text design: Frank Wiedemann
Cleis logo art: Juana Alicia
First Edition.
10 9 8 7 6 5 4 3

Contents

INTRODUCTION: MADE FOR SEX

Hotel rooms, in a word, are hot. The minute I enter one, I want to strip off all my clothes and dive naked between the sheets, whether I have a lover there to share in the indulgence with me or not. Much more so than my own bed, hotel beds make me horny. They are, or at least seem to me to be, made for sex.

Hotels give us the chance to unwind, relax, and, if we choose, become someone else. Behind closed doors, we are free to frolic, fuck, and flaunt ourselves. It doesn't matter whether the hotel is in a faraway land or in your own hometown; the point is, it's a clean slate. It's not your home filled with all the reminders of what you could or should be doing. Other people have fucked and will fuck in the bed you're about to sleep in; that can be a turn-on in and of itself. It's your borrowed space, for an hour, a day, a night, or longer, and in that time, you can claim it, control it, use it for your own naughty purposes. Other guests are prowling the hotel, checking in, checking out, banging and getting banged against the wall. There's a sense that anything can happen—and quite often, it does.

To me, the anonymity of hotel rooms, their personality wiped clean with each new guest, is part of their appeal. They beckon us with their welcoming ways. They offer an escape from the everyday, a chance to let loose and become someone else. In *Do Not Disturb,* I wanted to capture the ways hotels fit into our erotic imagination, whether they're a necessity or a luxury. Hotels let us explore parts of our passion that get left behind in the rush of daily life.

The authors whose work you are about to read understand perfectly the allure of a fresh hotel room—or a hotel lobby. Indeed, the entire atmosphere a hotel offers can simply scream of sex. This goes for five-star and by-the-hour joints. They each have something to add, and here you'll find romps between lovers and strangers—reunions or quickies—as these characters indulge in their new settings.

Many of the characters here use hotels for secrecy, relying on the unspoken code of employees to never share what goes on. Others use them for flirting, for catching their prey. Many need a hotel room in order to engage in an affair or a role-play. Whether exploring one of Japan's love hotels in Isabelle Gray's "So Simple a Place" or getting "A Room at the Grand" for a very special call girl, the men and women you'll read about get off on their surroundings. The hotel itself becomes a player in their affairs, a sign of the lengths they'll go to be together.

And this book wouldn't be complete without some examples of the extramarital affairs that can only happen in hotel rooms, like those of the lovers in Lisabet Sarai's "Reunion" or Gwen Masters's "Memphis." For these characters, the hotel room takes on added meaning for it is an ever-changing venue where their relationships grow, where they can savor each other's bodies without their spouses knowing, or so they hope.

Hotel rooms are also perfect for quickies, those fast fucks

that you only need an hour or so for, all the more arousing for their brevity. In Saskia Walker's "The Lunch Break," a sultry waitress pounces on a customer, and in my story "Hump Day," a couple shed their business personae once a week to become the kind of people they could never be (or fuck) at home.

Even in the more innocent stories here, the vacation sex, the getaways among couples, there's something just a little clandestine about these hotel room hookups. That air of perversion is what makes getting serviced in a hotel (or motel) infinitely sweeter than doing it anywhere else. It's a private way of being an exhibitionist, of leaving the staff and fellow guests guessing. Sometimes it's a temporary neighbor who'll lure you from the safety of your relationship, such as the lesbian who teaches Madlyn March's protagonist a thing or two in "Heart-Shaped Holes," or the fellow sequestered juror in Elizabeth Coldwell's "Guilty Pleasure" who helps a married lady relieve some tension in between trial time.

There's a hotel in New York, the Library Hotel, that has long intrigued me. They offer an Erotica Suite, filled with strawberries, whipped cream, red roses, erotic dice, Mionetto Prosecco, edible honey dust, and a *Kama Sutra* pocket guide. They're upfront in their intention that you truly savor their package, as well as your lover's. I've never stayed there, or done more than pass by. In some ways, I prefer to keep its beauty safely tucked away in my imagination, to imagine the kind of room I'd use with a rich lover from out of town who'd seduce me with his or her accent, whisper to me in a foreign tongue before taking that foreign tongue and licking me all over. That's another thing about hotel rooms: they are perfect to fantasize about. In them, and in your dreams about them, you can have any kind of sex with anyone (or everyone) you want.

I can tell you that the sex I've had in hotel rooms has been some of the hottest of my life. I get off on knowing that neighbors may hear me, and in fact, that brings out the exhibitionist in me. The sexiest porn director I know took me to his hotel room in Manhattan one night and while his porn star girlfriend was elsewhere, we indulged in one of the most dirty, powerful, delicious fucks I've ever had, and when he came all over my chest, I reveled in it. I didn't wash it off, either, but proudly let it dry on my skin and couldn't stop the smile that found its way to my lips as I took the subway home.

Once, in some random seedy L.A. hotel, another lover and I hadn't brought any condoms, and instead had to make do with a paddle and a butt plug—poor us. In a seedy Midtown motel, I spent a few hours romping with a very sexy young man who showed me all kinds of ways I could twist my body to extend my pleasure, then felt a shocked, naughty thrill as he entered the bathroom while I peed and watched me before dipping his fingers into the stream. Something I likely wouldn't have allowed at home became acceptable in a place I'd likely never find myself again. And when I'm in a hotel room by myself, tucked away under the sheets, I feel naughty and decadent, even if the only party guests I'm hosting are my fingers and my pussy.

While I doubt hotels are going to be stocking this book in their dresser drawers alongside the Bible, I hope that it finds its way into hotel romps. I picture lovers reading aloud to one another as they get ready to mark their hotel room, or in the afterglow, perhaps leaving it behind for the next lucky guest. I hope hotel staff spirit it away and read it during their downtime. I hope the next time you enter a hotel lobby, even if you have no intention of getting busy with anyone you may find there, you'll at least notice the many erotic possibilities that greet you.

My most recent hotel rendezvous was at the ultrafancy art-filled Chambers Hotel in Minneapolis. I was staying by myself for two nights, and while I didn't share my bed, the room itself beckoned to me. I found myself getting horny as I slid between the covers, wishing I had a lover to share my good fortune with. Now I have this book, which I hope you'll take with you on your travels and perhaps read it while lounging in a hotel lobby, or whisper from it into your lover's ear before you make so much noise in your hotel room bed that someone calls security. However and wherever you read this book, I hope it turns you on as much as it does me.

Rachel Kramer Bussel
New York City

WELCOME TO THE APHRODISIAC HOTEL

Amanda Earl

I've always had a thing for hotel lobby bars. They act as a buffer between business and pleasure. Sometimes business is pleasure. I shiver with desire in the shadow of a group of bankers or politicians sipping their scotch, the scent of money and power folded into every crease of their navy blue suits. Do these men have mistresses or escorts waiting for them in their luxury suites? Maybe a bellboy will kneel for them after he takes their luggage up to their rooms, for a little money in his palm. Or perhaps basking in the afterglow of a strategic win is all they need, sitting in this bar, nursing their drinks. They never seem in any hurry to leave.

These establishments have their own sets of rules—check your morality at the door along with your suitcase. When you visit a hotel lobby bar, anything can happen. What I like about them is their illicitness, the fact that they are just steps away from elevators that carry clandestine lovers up to hotel beds where so many other people have fucked or cried or indulged in decadent room service dinners. Or maybe it's their transitory nature…places where strangers pass in the night for one brief encounter that could change their lives forever—or at least for right now.

The woman sitting at the wrought iron and marble table for two near the window and sipping a dry martini with two olives is a sales rep, most likely for a pharmaceutical company. There are numerous drug sales reps in hotel lobby bars at any given moment.

I notice her the moment she walks in. I muse over whether she's a blatant or merely accidental exhibitionist. Her beige skirt is made of some deceptive material that becomes translucent if the light hits it at the right angle. I wonder if she realizes. I wonder if she knows that when she's giving her presentation to the medical community with a white screen behind her that she's showing off a small black triangle of fabric that barely covers her private parts. Maybe she does know and it turns her on. I bet she'd love to do something about that. I can tell by the way she keeps shifting in her seat and touching her body.

She's placed her matching jacket neatly over the chair back. It has no wrinkles and she's the type who wants to keep it that way, I'll wager. I wonder about her uncreased life. What would it take to rumble it up? I watch her remove her shoes—each a respectable few inches of heel and a closed toe—and massage her feet briefly. I doubt she's into feet, though. Foot sluts wear open-toed shoes. She's probably been standing all day, what with the presentation and the glad-handing at exhibitors' booths.

She stretches her nylon-clad calves and rubs the balls of her feet along the rich blue carpeting, just for a moment, then she frowns and slips her feet back into the shoes. I'm sure she'd love for a man to kneel and massage those tired dogs and gams for her, maybe let his hand move up along those supple thighs, reach in between. She squirms in her seat. I feel like I'm reading her mind.

She's rubbed her eyes twice now and she's almost finished that martini. This is the face of a woman who's seen many a hotel room. This is one of those newfangled boutique hotels, big city whatsitsname's attempt at sophistication and panache. But you can tell she isn't impressed. She doesn't have the look of wonder of someone easily fooled. She isn't beaming at the view that's supposed to make guests feel privileged. She isn't ordering the overpriced chicken on a stick, nor has she made small talk with the waiter when he's come by to take her order. She's reading the fine print of some pill dispenser and checking it against a list, likely an inventory.

Her life is ordered, prearranged with appointments and meetings. She stretches, undoes the top button of her blouse, then another. Finally able to loosen up a bit now that she's not the center of attention, she rolls her neck and massages it, then takes a gulp of her drink. This woman desperately needs to let go of all that tension between her shoulders and in her brain. The drink is having its effect though.

A tall man in a tattered sports jacket and faded corduroy slacks carries his medical bag into the bar. He shakes his shaggy blond hair, and I notice those California baby blues for the first time. I bet beneath that staid sports jacket and corduroys is a body any woman would love to get her hands on. His tie is knotted loosely, not quite all the way up to the top of his shirt neck. I can see tufts of chest hair, just peeking out. He has the kind of torso that makes me think he's in good shape too. What woman doesn't like the shy, handsome type?

He heads to a table near a group of businessmen guffawing loudly and sputtering beer saliva at one another, grabbing handfuls of peanuts, making googly eyes at the breasts of the waitress as she leans forward to pick up their empty steins. I'm sure at least one of them thinks he's going to have her for the night. By the vacant look in her eyes and the fake smile on her face, I can tell she's served men like this for years.

I know her name is Beth because I've chatted with her before in this bar, but I think of her as Elizabeth. That long, elegant neck was meant for diamonds and her graceful, sinewy body for love-making all night long beneath silk sheets. Instead, she's schlepping beer to these losers. I admire her dancer's legs as she walks to the next table, looking more like she's floating than walking.

How many men have tried to hit on her here? Maybe she's even indulged herself a time or two for a brief encounter, letting some well-spoken foreign diplomat lead her into his room and worship her beautiful breasts, undo the flimsy elastic band holding up her glistening blonde hair to let it cascade over her soft, naked shoulders as he whispers in French about all the different ways he's going to fuck her. I'd like to see Elizabeth let go, let herself be taken, her lips swollen and bruised with kisses.

Perhaps she'd be a great match for our doctor. Maybe the two of them could unleash that quiet fire I can see in their cool blue eyes. But he doesn't stay in her serving area, thanks to the loud boors. He chooses to sit in the tall wingback chair facing the sales rep and pulls out his papers, which take flight and land at the feet of our sales rep, whose name I've decided is Ms. Mavis Blackstone.

Ms. Blackstone leans over and both the doctor and I catch a glimpse of her freckled peach décolletage. In the process of leaning over, she tips the glass and spills what's left of her drink onto the marble tabletop, sending the glass tumbling to the floor and splashing vermouth on the corduroyed hem of our doctor's pants.

Both she and the doctor cry out. How well they harmonize.

What would they sound like in the crescendo of their mutual orgasms as he slams into her over and over again and she spreads herself wide on the scratchy hotel sheets, letting her body merge into the spongy queen-sized mattress, both of them screaming so loudly the guest in the next room bangs on the walls?

Her face turns red as she mumbles an apology for spilling her drink on the doctor. When she hands him the papers, also dotted with alcohol, their hands touch, just for an instant. The electricity between them sparks in their fingers, travels from the pulse of their wrists, courses along their bloodstreams and zings, zapping them both right in the groin. I can feel it from my seat at the bar. Must have been at least a 4.1 on the arousal scale.

It's the doctor's turn to look embarrassed and shift his body so that our young Ms. Blackstone does not see the erection rapidly developing beneath his faded corduroy trousers. At this point the waiter arrives.

He's a new waiter and I haven't had the chance to fantasize about him yet—probably a college student, making money for school. I love his short curly dark hair, wonder what it would be like to see that luxuriant head of hair between my legs, as he licks at my cunt. Perhaps he enjoys older women. It's clear he's in good shape, thanks to the tight hotel regulation uniform slacks that display his sweet little ass so well.

I want to rub my hands over the zipper, watch how his erection flares at the mere touch of my hand through the fabric. In a soft and sultry voice, he asks the doctor for his drink order. The quiet tones of his syllables whisper over my skin. I can feel my nipples hardening beneath my silk blouse. I'm watching others but I look around briefly and wonder just who might be watching me. That thought sends a jolt of arousal between my legs.

Dr. Miles Jones, as I've decided to call him, orders the sales rep another drink and tells the waiter he'll have what Ms.

Blackstone is having. Ms. Blackstone is still red with embarrassment, causing the freckles on her face and chest to become more visible. By the glazed look in his eyes, I can tell Dr. Jones has never seen anything more desirable than this embarrassed freckled woman.

She goes back to her inventory procedure, her hand trembling as she ticks off medicines. He pulls random objects from his medical bag: a prescription pad, a pocket watch. I'm expecting him to pull out a rabbit soon. Eventually he finds what he's looking for, a map of the city. This is a smooth maneuver on his part to engage Ms. Blackstone in conversation. Play the tourist. It's from Dating 101. I am awed. I hadn't expected the gangly Dr. Jones to be this suave.

Wait, though, what's that on his finger? Damn. Looks like a wedding ring. Ms. Blackstone has seen it too. Yet she doesn't let that stop her. In fact, she continues to chat with our Dr. Jones.

Soon the two are seated at her table, his corduroy trousers pressing against her nylon-clad legs as she squirms in her seat. He's looking into her eyes. She's fiddling with her cocktail stick. I notice a shiny diamond on her finger. She twists it around a few times. Takes a bit of her long auburn hair and plays with it, then slips the end between her lips.

I wonder how many more signals Dr. Jones will need before he understands that this woman wants him to take her to bed. She touches his arm. That's the one. He finally understands and gestures to the waiter for the bill. Is it my imagination or does the waiter look on with envy? Does the waitress? I know I do.

The couple rises and leaves the room, his hand caressing the small of her back as they walk to the bank of elevators that will take them up to one of the bedrooms. I wonder whose room they will decide on. I contemplate the erection I've glimpsed between Dr. Jones's legs and the wet spot in the crease of Ms.

Blackstone's thin skirt, the tiny drop of perspiration on her lip as she smiles.

The man I've arranged to hook up with has just arrived. He's not our blond doctor, he's a dark-haired beauty with flecks of silver in his hair. I don't need to use my imagination to know what happens next. I whisper in his ear and we go straight to the elevators. As usual, the theater of lust acted out in the hotel lobby bar has turned me on. I need no further foreplay than that.

TIGHTLY TUCKED

Alison Tyler

Elian Mitchell used hotels.

He used them the way some meticulous people use up every last bit of toothpaste in a tube of Colgate, pressing the metal flat and then rolling up the end to make sure not a smear goes to waste.

Elian used the minibar, reveling in the tiny bottles of liquor. He often wondered why drinks made from miniature bottles tasted better, more luxurious somehow, than ones poured from a full-size container.

He used the endless hot water supply, showering up to three times in a single day, filling the rooms with billows of white steam, not paying attention where he left the towels afterward. Because without a doubt, one of Elian's favorite things about staying in a hotel was using the maid service. This pleasure ran deeper than his little fetish for girls with feather dusters—no matter how obsolete he understood that image might have been. You see, the best part about hotel life to Elian was not worrying.

Did he leave those fluffy white terry-cloth towels draped over the back of the armchair?

Maybe.

Or were they in a heap beneath the sink?

Perhaps.

If he emptied the minibar, someone was available at the push of a square red button to bring him exactly what he needed. If he abused every last towel, he could call down and request more.

At home, he was expected to refold the towels and place them back on the rack when he was through. This was called common courtesy by his brand-new girlfriend, and he understood Sophie's point. She didn't want to have to pick up after him any more than he wanted to pick up after her.

But on the road, one of the perks was that lack of consideration.

Sophie, however, could not seem to get the hang of hotel life. She tsked softly to herself when she found a smudge in the corner of the large mirror. Elian had been hoping to fuck Sophie in front of the mirror, to strip her out of her traveling clothes and make love to her right on the floor. He would have, too, if Sophie hadn't been so damn busy. Busy tsking.

Elian had heard from a college friend that all couples ought to take a vacation together before deciding whether they were destined for success. So far, Sophie hadn't wowed him with her traveling abilities, but he had learned a few things about her. He learned that she was the type to unpack every last item in her suitcase before settling down, the type to stroke the remote with an antiseptic wipe she'd brought from home. The type who apparently couldn't relax even when relaxation was the only item on their agenda.

By the time she was finished with her evening routine, she

said she was too tired to move. Elian jacked off quietly in the bed at her side, imagining Sophie stripped down on all fours in the center of the rumpled covers and what he would do to her.

"They don't even make the bed right," Sophie muttered before she rolled over. "I like my sheets tightly tucked."

In the morning, Elian hoped to woo Sophie to what he considered the sweet debauchery of hotel living. He wanted to laze in bed for hours, to call room service for Eggs Benedict and mimosas, to get French bread crumbs in the bed. Crumbs he wouldn't have to worry about, because some nameless, faceless maid would magically produce fresh white sheets by the time they returned from sightseeing.

If Sophie could only see how fun eating toast in bed was, maybe she'd agree to munch on buttered scones every so often in his bed at home.

But by the time Elian awoke, Sophie was dressed and waiting for him. Not only did she seem anxious for him to get dressed, but for him to physically move, so that she could remake the bed. He didn't understand at first what she was asking, but slowly the concept seeped into his pre-caffeinated brain: to Elian's dismay, Sophie was actually going to clean their room before the maid arrived.

"I don't want her to think we're slobs," Sophie said, neatly folding even the few washcloths that she'd used.

"That's her job," Elian said softly as he pulled on a pair of jeans.

"To think we're slobs?"

"To clean up," Elian replied through clenched teeth. He couldn't even look at his girlfriend. Had he actually wanted to fuck her last night? Now, when she got close, he thought he smelled that antiseptic wipe she used on everything. Was there ever a moment when Sophie wasn't clean smelling, freshly washed, minty tasting?

"Let's just go," Elian said, hand on the door, watching while Sophie made the bed. He was enjoying their hotel stay less and less, although he did have to admire how well Sophie was able to create those neat hospital corners with the sheets. She refused to be rushed, and when she was finished, the room looked as pristine as it had upon check-in. Even cleaner, Elian thought to himself, because Sophie had gotten on her hands and knees to pick up a few specks of lint in one corner.

He felt the beginning of a headache shoot through his temples as he watched her write a note to the maid, then place the folded square with a five dollar bill on the dresser.

If she was going to do such a thorough job, at least she could wear the cute little maid outfit he'd bought her for Valentine's Day. But she'd told him the outfit—as well as the fantasy—was demeaning, and she had brought the flouncy uniform back to the store.

When they returned from sightseeing, Elian discovered that the maid had left a note of her own:

> *Thank you very much for the tip.*
> *You don't need to make the bed since I change the sheets every day.*
> *—Bella*

He showed the note to Sophie, who announced in her haughtiest tone that she didn't care. She'd make the bed anyway. And she did. Every day. Tightly tucking the sheets, going on her knees to pick up any stray bits of fluff, creating a home away from home.

A home Elian wasn't sure he liked.

* * *

On their final day, an unexpected downpour proved that weathermen are not omniscient. "We don't have to sightsee every single moment," Elian said. He could feel himself getting excited. The rain meant that they could stay in, order room service, maybe watch a little porn on the TV. "Part of the vacation is meant to be spent just relaxing," Elian continued.

Sophie was having none of that. She had the same way of speaking as his second grade teacher, a teacher who'd brooked no horseplay. "None of that," she'd say, with a way of pursing her lips in disapproval that made Elian feel dirty.

"Just move, so I can make the bed," she insisted, and rather than argue, Elian perched on the armchair and watched. Hospital corners. Sheets so taut you could bounce a quarter off the center. Tightly tucked, just the way Sophie liked them.

"I'm not going," Elian said. If Sophie was going to act like a schoolmarm, then Elian was going to respond by being a brat. He couldn't help himself. He wished he had a slingshot.

Once she had the room spotless once more, Sophie took her camera and the rain slicker she'd brought just in case (of course), and left Elian alone. Oh, thank fucking god. Alone. For the first time in five days, he was by himself. Immediately, and with the glee of a kid playing hooky, he stripped off the counterpane and jumped on the bed. He bounced for a few minutes before rolling off the mattress like a puppy and rearranging all of the furniture in the room. He was gleeful, beside himself with the pleasure that he always felt when staying at hotels. Finally, he remembered exactly why he liked to travel. He pulled open the minibar and made himself a Bloody Mary, then watched a good hour and a half of porn before falling asleep.

Elian was in a heavy dreamy daze when a knock on the door woke him. He decided that Sophie must have forgotten her key—although if he'd been all the way awake, he would have realized how unlike Sophie that would have been. Yawning, he stumbled to the latch, wearing only his gray sweats and sporting a sleep-hardened erection. In the hallway stood the maid, pert and perfectly adorable, with short curly blonde hair and clear, blue eyes. She took one look at Elian and said, "You're not the one making the fucking bed, are you?"

Elian smiled.

This wasn't a girl who would have said no to a French maid outfit. He'd only just met her, but he was sure. If he were to buy her vinyl, or leather, or schoolgirl plaid, she would slide into any fantasy confection with no more hesitation than it took to shoot him a wicked grin. The same wicked one she was giving him now.

Elian took a step back and invited her in. Something in his attitude must have let her know what he wanted, and she obliged, leaving her cart in the hall. There was no discussion about what he wanted from her, no need to press the red square button to get what he was after. Bella came easily into his arms, a lithe, athletic body that he lifted in an automatic embrace. He kissed her mouth, then her freckled cheeks, then nibbled on her earlobes. He moved her with him into the bathroom and they took a shower together, getting warm and wet and soapy, laughing as they dried each other off.

Oh, she was so different from Sophie. Sophie who wouldn't get her hair wet, because the water would make her chestnut waves turn frizzy. Sophie who folded each towel neatly after patting herself dry. Elian watched as Bella dropped the towels in a soggy heap on the floor, and he wanted to go on his knees right then on the slippery white tiles and propose. Instead, the two were halfway to the bed before he grabbed her and threw her down on the plush, crimson carpeting that Sophie had picked lint off of on her hands and knees. He moved Bella on top of him into a still-damp sixty-nine.

She might not have been aces with a vacuum, but the girl knew how to use her tongue, sliding the tip along his cock in a dreamy way while dragging her nails against his skin.

Elian followed her lead, tickling her inner thighs while keeping his mouth busy on her cunt. He breathed in deep, focusing on the way she tasted, clean from the shower, of course, but musky beneath—earthy and real and delicious. Her fragrance was rich and heady and entirely unlike the antiseptic flavor of Sophie's well-douched vagina. Sophie never really liked sixty-nining. She would suck Elian *occasionally* when requested, but she pushed him away when he tried to go down on her.

How odd, he thought now, that Sophie seemed to prefer going down on her hands and knees and picking microscopic specs off the carpet to going down on him.

He lapped at Bella with no thought of what she was doing to his cock. He was lost within the walls of her pussy, drinking each drop of her sweetness. When he felt he was on the verge of coming, he pushed thoughts of his own pleasure away, moving so that he was out of her reach, lying flat on the floor between her legs and concentrating totally on giving her pleasure. She wrapped her slim, strong thighs around him and let him work, whispering what she wanted, how she liked it.

"Harder," she groaned, when she needed more pressure, "faster, ohhh, please, faster," and he made those spiraling little circles as quickly as he could until she pressed her hips forward and drenched his lips with the juices of her climax. The taste was sublime, like the first drop of whiskey from a tiny minibar bottle.

By the time Sophie arrived back at the hotel, Bella and Elian were on their second beer. Sophie didn't know what to make of the scene, so Elian told her. "You're doing Bella's job. Cleaning. Folding. Making the bed. So I invited her to do yours...kick back, relax, make love."

Only moments later, Sophie left with her very neatly folded clothes in her suitcase. Bella and Elian had another beer, then climbed back beneath the tightly tucked sheets.

FROM RUSSIA WITH LUST

Stan Kent

I travel a lot. So many airports, so many hotel rooms, so many boring business meals—the novelty of being sent to an exotic location soon wears off. Yes, there are the perks. Millions of frequent flyer miles I'll never use, fast track through screening and passport control, some very cool shopping opportunities, and the chance to time a trip at exactly the same time that a very special, once-in-a-lifetime concert is happening. What a coincidence! Imagine that. How fortunate that the customer needed a meeting that simply couldn't be handled any other way than face-to-face. And speaking of the personal touch, there's always the chance when traveling of a fleeting encounter of the sexy kind. I'm not talking about a rip-off lap dance designed to separate you from those expense report dollars carefully disguised as "Miscellaneous Snacks," but a collision of bodies, an exchange of passions where strangers meet and end up something more, if only for an hour or two one night before that early morning flight back home.

In all my years of globe-trotting, however, I must say that such experiences are rare. I can count them on my fingers. Let's see, there was that time in Sydney—that was her name and it was the town, talk about synchronicity—and then there was Tonje from Oslo, and, oh, yeah that one night in Bangkok, and well now I mention it there was that time in the Arctic Circle and the Japanese students at the Ice Hotel, and how could I forget the birds from Birmingham—England, not Alabama—okay, maybe fingers and toes will be needed to keep track, but don't get the wrong impression from my open kimono time. I'm not a jet-set lothario. When measured against the hundreds of trips I've taken, these few business trip bonks are like winning the lottery. Most of the time the release of sexual tension is a quick wank in the hotel room to whatever passes for porn in that part of the world.

And so it goes. I was in Moscow nearing the end of a long winter trip. I was tired from the endless negotiations that Russians are expert at prolonging; too tired to go to the Tsunami, the local titty bar, for a lap dance or perhaps even a backroom private session. That's how tired I was. Mentally beat, so I flicked on the tube and beat my meat to pay-for-view Russki porn which was actually from Germany. It was a kinky little number, the title of which somehow got lost in translation from German to Russian to English as *Down the Long Deep Dark Tunnel*. It was about a woman whose clitoris was up her butt—a Euro-anal rip-off of *Deep Throat*, but done with a fine attention to fetish, with the lifting up of leather skirts and the pulling down of glowing pink thong panties and white seamed tights, all in skyscraper tall Nu-Rock platform boots with much gyrating and head tossing of fluorescent hair, all done to a booming Teutonic techno soundtrack—tasty.

I was lying on the bed naked, stroking away, almost at the point of no return, when I noticed that the curtains weren't quite drawn. The hotel was an intimate courtyard affair and all the rooms faced each other so it was very easy to see into other rooms when the lights were on. It was the dark, dark Russian winter, and I was enjoying my virtual trip Down the Long Deep Dark Tunnel, but a slight sense of modesty, or perhaps embarrassment, overcame me. I wasn't ashamed so much as worried that someone would think I was a loser for wanking to hotel porn when in Russia there are many willing Natashas to ease the traveler's burden. Call me vain, but I got up, while not missing a beat, to close the drapes.

Now there is one thing I've noticed that all my frequent traveler fuckings have had in common. They all happen when I'm least expecting it. All the good stuff, the winning of the licentious lottery, happens when I'm not looking for it, when I don't bother buying a ticket for the casual sex sweepstakes. I'm usually rushing here or there and a hottie happens to bend to straighten her stockings, and I notice her Christian Louboutins and Wolfords, and I pay her a compliment on her choice of leg and foot coverings and then life gets interesting. It's that chance encounter that simply can't happen when you're on the hunt. That's why titty bars can be frustrating and require so much investment for the slim chance of any return.

But I digress: back to the crack in the drapes. As much as I didn't want to take my eyes off my kinky fräulein being rear-ended, I had to glance to make sure I grabbed the curtain. I was, after all, doing this job with one hand. My head turned from the porn on the screen to the cracked curtains, and I had a revelation on the road to modesty: I saw real-life porn on a hotel bed. There they were, fucking doggie-style in the room directly opposite and one floor down. I had a perfect view because their drapes were wide open. They were putting on a show. I suddenly lost interest in my five-hundred ruble movie discreetly billed to the hotel room as an expense report "communications" charge. I turned out my lights and opened the drapes wide enough for me to watch unhindered and wank freely to the live show I'd stumbled upon.

The exhibitionist couple looked like the typical nu-Russian pairing. She was young, no more than twenty-five, and was supermodel gorgeous with legs from here to the Kremlin, while he was beer-bellied, boxy, and in his thirties. Natasha had long black hair that draped Cleopatra-like over her shoulders and swished in time to Boris's poundings. I had no idea if Boris and Natasha were my porn show couple's names, but I needed to call them something and that was as good as anything. He looked like a Boris and she sure had the Natasha thing down. Her breasts weren't large—two taut cones with large nipples—yes, I could see that much detail—that rippled more than swung with each thrust, her hair thoughtfully swishing forward to peekaboo her tits. She was tight and fit, with no trace of the ravages of the bad diet that will many years later most probably ruin her fuck-able looks.

Even though Boris's body showed signs of one too many Baltika beers, he had staying power, I'll give him that. More than me. Weeks of no nookie and too much stimulation had taken their toll. I came on the window, my legs buckled, and I fell back into an easy chair. Once I'd come down from coming, I grabbed a tissue, wiped the spunky stream away, and settled in to watch the show.

And what a show it was.

Boris pulled on Natasha's hair with a gripped fist. Her back arched, her head angled back, her neck stretched taut. She looked to be moaning. His face was contorted and red. Sweat glistened on his forehead. Natasha reached under her, between her legs, to bring herself off, I fancied, but no, she went farther and grabbed

Boris's balls and squeezed. I swear I saw red nails bite into his flesh. His head went back and he opened his mouth to bay and thrust in hard and stayed there at the hilt with Natasha milking the come from him.

He collapsed forward and they fell into the bed, exhausted, I imagined.

I was hard again.

My bought porn movie had ended. What was I to do? Another five-hundred ruble "communications" charge, or should I get dressed and go looking for the real thing?

Or maybe the free porn show wasn't over.

Natasha and Boris had rolled over. She licked his softening cock, which pretty soon turned into a hardening cock. Her moon-shaped ass and snow white thighs were toward me. I leaned forward to see the pout of her pussy, and then she turned and straddled him and rode him into her screaming climax, pulling on her tits as her hair slashed across her body like so many tiny whips.

I was still hard. My previous wank had been mere foreplay. Now I wasn't so hair-triggered. I could savor the sexy sight before me as I slowly, slowly played with my sensitized cock, expecting more sexual fireworks, but Boris and Natasha had cooled. They lolled together on the bed, no doubt toasting each other's sexual prowess with vodka. Soon, Boris got up and snapped off the light. I was still hard. I kept watching and hoping that they'd start up again. Every little shadowy movement suggested sex, but my exhibitionist lovers must have been worn out. I got up from my catbird seat and crawled into bed. I was still hard. I fell asleep hard. I woke up hard and went over to the window to see if Boris and Natasha were having morning sex.

The curtains were drawn.

My day with customers dragged. My mind was on hotel room 428—that was the number—I couldn't resist nailing down the location as I left for my appointments. I went down one floor and walked around, counting the rooms until I was even with mine. I'd hoped to run into Boris and Natasha, but they must have been sleeping in. A DO NOT DISTURB sign hung on their door. They were sleeping the rest of the well fucked and I, in stark opposition to their Do Not Disturb state, was very definitely Disturbed by their performance. Look at me, I was stalking them! I could not get their fucking out of my mind. This was like Hitchcock's *Rear Window* with sex, and I was an obsessed, perverted, and horny Jimmy Stewart. I wished I could have spent all day in the room, watching, waiting for the curtains to open. What I would have done I'm not sure, but that didn't matter.

I was wound tight. I made excuses to my clients that I had to have a telecon with the States and it being Friday afternoon in Moscow, why didn't we call it an early day and resume on Monday? They agreed; I couldn't wait to get back to the hotel. I worried all the way through crowded Russian streets that Boris and Natasha might have checked out. I was sweating like a junkie needing to score. I couldn't wait for the next installment; there had to be another session. It couldn't end like this. I was in such a rush to get to my room that I almost missed them. They were in the bar. Boris was talking loudly on a cell phone, sipping on a whisky, and Natasha drank champagne and looked bored but drop-dead gorgeous, the way fashion models have perfected. I spun around, claimed a bar stool as my own, ordered a bottle of Russian Standard vodka, and angled myself so I could watch them in the mirror above the bar.

They'd been shopping. Dolce and Gabbana, Gucci, and Versace seemed to have been hit pretty hard judging by the mountain of bags sitting next to Natasha's shapely legs, which were today covered in black Wolford stockings. I knew they were stockings because Boris had his hand on Natasha's thigh. As he blabbered into his phone, he absentmindedly squeezed her thigh, causing her little black dress to ride upward enough to reveal that delectable vision of black stocking top meeting pale white thigh. My reaction was Pavlovian. My cock stirred in my pants, and I took a strong shot of icy cold Russian Standard.

They went through several more drinks, and I knocked back many a Russian Standard. I was feeling very warm and fuzzy when Natasha got up from the table. She swung her legs to the side and Boris's hand slipped away, pulling the dress to the side. In the bar mirror I saw that thin strip of hair up closer than I'd seen last night. She wasn't wearing any panties—just black stockings and a garter belt. The vision was momentary, but the impression was lasting. I knew then I had to get out of there or risk trouble. There are lots of guys like Boris in Moscow, and they're mostly mob related. It fit—the Mob Guy and his Moll, and I might find myself falling from a high building if I did anything to piss him off, like stick my head up Natasha's skirt and eat her pussy while he was preoccupied with his call.

Trust me; I've had enough Russian Standard to know it is a premium foolish behavior enabler. It's just too good and smooth and slides down easy just like I could slide down easy all over Natasha. *Oh, crap, I've got to get out of here.* I paid my bill, charging it to my room where it would appear as "snacks and refreshments" for a meeting with a client, and how I wished Natasha was my clitty client.

I took the rest of the bottle in hand and turned to go to the elevators. Just as I did, Natasha returned and gave Boris a demanding look. He snapped something into his phone and clicked it shut. He got up, threw a bunch of rubles on the table, took Natasha's arm in one hand and all the bags in another, and headed for the elevator. I followed, enjoying the view of

Natasha's lithe frame strutting in her wispy A-line black dress. And she had no panties on. It was all I could do to stop myself from dropping to the floor and slithering along behind them like some perverted python looking up those legs, past the stockings to that curve of her tight little butt and the pinkness between her legs that would wink at me with every step.

Yeah, Russian Standard is a dangerous thing.

The elevator came quickly, which, if I had mounted Natasha right then, so would I have. They went in first and I followed, standing to the side of Natasha. I kept telling myself: *She's a foot away from me and not wearing any panties. Last night I saw her being fucked and fucking.* And then I cooled my jets, noticing that big bad Boris was just two more feet away from me. I looked down at my feet, but that made me look at her feet. Stocking-covered toes peeked through open-toed Casadei stilettos. And then there were Boris's feet next to Natasha's, in expensive Gucci loafers. Definitely the Mob. I looked away quickly to the floor counter. We were at four. Boris looked at me and smiled. What to do? Was this an invitation to join them? He nodded at the half empty bottle of Russian Standard and said, "*Na zdorovia.*" Cheers, or more precisely, to your health. I was tempted to look at Natasha and say "*Na zdorovia*" because I'd have loved to toast a sip of her randy Russian pussy.

But I didn't. I raised the bottle and said, "Cheers." Natasha got out first, followed by Boris. He grabbed her ass and she giggled. They ran to their room. I hit the CLOSE button on the elevator and pounded on the FIVE button even though it was already lit. It took what I thought was forever to reach five, and I was through the doors before they were fully open. I sprang into the room after fumbling with the in-and-out of the electronic key until finally I got it in right, and isn't that a metaphor for how flustered I felt? I threw the lights on, ran over to my catbird seat, opened the drapes, and took a shot of Russian Standard from the bottle.

Na zdorovia indeed. The lights were on in 428 and Boris and Natasha were definitely home. She was lying on the bed, spread wide legs bent at the knee. The dress was gone; all she had on were her stockings, garter belt, stilettos, and a blissed-out smile as a fully clothed Boris buried his face in her cunt. His arms were around her thighs, pulling her onto his tongue. Her head rolled from side to side; her hair was splayed around the bed like a deep black pool. This was good stuff. I took a swig of Russian Standard and stood up. I wasn't sure why, but perhaps it was that a performance like what I was being treated to needed acknowledging. Who knows, maybe this whole side of the hotel was glued to their windows, wanking away to the Boris and Natasha show. So I stood up and took a few steps toward the window, staying just far enough back that my breath didn't mist up the view. I took a swig of vodka, and as I turned my head to look back, Natasha's head rolled to face me. Our eyes met. There was contact. She appeared to moan, and she kept looking at me. She smiled and moaned again. I felt like I was in that sex-filled room hearing Boris's lapping of Natasha's cunt, smelling the lust dripping from her—from Russia with lust.

With my free hand (I wasn't going to put my Russian Standard down) I unzipped my pants and took out my cock. I stroked it and took another swig of vodka—it was my Russian courage, giving me the balls to be so brazen, because if Natasha could see me, so could anyone else on that side of the hotel. I tried to put that thought and the possible consequences of being arrested in Russia for indecent exposure out of my mind and focus on room 428. Natasha was all eyes, big and round on me. She wasn't rolling her head from side to side; she was watching me jerk off. She opened her mouth and licked her lips, her pink tongue smearing her bright red lipstick. She kept her mouth open as if she were ready to take my cock into her throat as Boris licked her pussy.

Boris! I'd almost forgotten about him. He was still between Natasha's legs, licking away, but one of his hands had slipped from holding her thigh and was finger-fucking her. From the angle, it looked like he was giving her a good G-spot workout. Old Boris, he knew his stuff. It didn't take long for this kind of intense finger and tongue working in sync to bring her off. Her back arched. Her spiked heels dug deep into the bed. Her fingers squeezed her breasts. Our eyes made contact and then she shut them tight as she came. I was close to coming but I held back. I'd watched her come; I wanted to repay the favor. She relaxed back into the bed. Her hands flopped to her sides. I took another swig of Russian Standard. Her mouth closed. She caught her breath. She opened her eyes and looked at me, and my cock. She blew me a kiss. I blew her one back, and then I blew my load onto the window. It was my turn to close my eyes and moan in pure, visceral ecstasy. The rush was unbelievable, a melting warmth spreading up my legs and into my head. I felt like I was passing out. Whoops—I was. It was drunken coming. Before I lost consciousness, I opened my eyes. Boris and Natasha were sitting on the bed, smiling, looking at me. They waved. I lifted the bottle to them, mouthed *Na zdorovia,* and took one last swig of Russian Standard.

Then I passed out, falling back into the catbird seat, where I slept in my suit. There I stayed throughout the night, my head pounding so loud it sounded like someone was knocking on my door. I woke uncomfortably when the stark winter sun broke through the clouds and blasted the snow-covered grounds. My head still pounded as if someone was knocking on my door. My cock was sticking out of my trousers. My mouth was dry. A mighty big stream of spunk trailed down the window. The curtains to 428 were open but nobody was in the room. I looked at the clock. It was almost noon. Good thing I didn't have any early meetings that day because it was Saturday. I decided to take a shower. I got up, and as I made my way to the bathroom I noticed an envelope that had been pushed through the door. I bent to pick it up and almost kissed the carpet, I felt so dizzy. My head was like lead. I fell to the floor on my knees and opened the letter. It read in halting English:

> *Dear Kinky Guy in Room 527:*
>
> *Hello. We hope we not disturb you with our knocking on your door, but we want you to join us for much hot sex. But no answer. We sad because we must leave early today but happy because we will be at this hotel in exactly one month. We want you join us for hot sex. I want you to screw my wife with me. You look like kinky guy we looking for. Other peoples looked but you only one to show your cock. Email us if you into a troika.*
>
> *Na zdorovia,*
> *Vlad and Eva*

Damn that Russian Standard. If I hadn't drunk so much I could have been down there instead of down here on my knees. But wait...exactly one month...I could arrange a meeting in Moscow, no problem.

As I mentioned in the beginning, that's one of the perks of being a frequent business traveler, and what happened when I returned to Russia with Lust exactly one month later is another tale to be added to my growing list of frequent traveler fuckings. *Na zdorovia.*

MIRROR, MIRROR

Andrea Dale

When Callista pulled up in front of the hotel, Evan looked at her quizzically.

"We both live within half an hour of here," he pointed out.

"True," she said. "But I've got something special in mind."

She checked them in, and they headed up to the room. If the concierge noticed they had no luggage, he made no comment.

The room was beautifully appointed in rich blues and golds. The sheets of the king-sized four-poster bed were turned down, a chocolate on each pillow. The fruit basket on the table near the window was the last thing they were interested in.

Because what made the room really special were the mirrors.

The walls at the head and across from the foot of the bed were mirrored, as was the ceiling above.

She turned to Evan, put her arms around him, and drew him into a slow, intimate dance.

"Now we have our own private space, just the two of us, to

watch…and be watched." She reached up, ran her thumb over Evan's sensual lower lip. "Have you ever watched yourself make love, Evan?" she asked huskily. "It's incredibly erotic."

"I'd rather watch you," he said, his own voice hoarse. He tugged her finger into his mouth and sucked. The wet warmth, the gentle rhythm, created a slow, delicious ache in her groin.

"So let's watch both of us and see what happens," she said.

She turned him to face the mirror at the foot of the bed. Standing behind him, her cheek resting on his upper arm, she reached around and began unbuttoning his shirt. One button at a time, revealing a widening V of hair-dusted flesh. She tugged the shirt free from his waistband and pulled it apart.

She drifted her fingers along the edges of his shirt, tracing the muscles of his chest; splayed out her palms to savor the warmth of his skin; trailed her fingertips in smaller and smaller circles around his nipples. All the while, she watched his expression in the mirror, admiring the way his eyes darkened, liking the way his chest moved with his sharp intake of breath when she reached the center of her spiral motion.

She'd already learned his nipples were sensitive but not in a bad way. She captured each one between her nails and plucked gently.

His hips jerked.

Breaking eye contact, she allowed herself to look down his body. His cock made a clear outline in his slacks. Yes, he was definitely enjoying this. She looked back up.

"It's a different perspective, isn't it?" she murmured. "Watching it happen to you. Over there, as if it's happening to someone else, but you can still feel every second of it."

He caught her wrists. "I want to feel you."

"I thought you'd never ask." She stepped away from him, off to one side so he had to turn to watch her. She teased him with her shirt, pulling it up a little, dropping it again, before finally easing it over her head. She didn't make him wait too long for the bra to go, toying with one strap for a moment and letting it slide down her arm before she unhooked the garment and let it drop to the floor.

Then she moved to stand in front of him, close, so that his erection snuggled against the crack of her ass. Even with slacks and skirt and underwear between them, she swore she could feel the heat radiating from him.

She wiggled her hips just a little, to feel him press against her, rubbing. "Mm, nice fit." She caught his gaze in the mirror. "Touch me," she said.

He skimmed his wide hands across her rib cage, and she watched, fascinated and aroused by the sight of his long fingers against her flesh. His warm touch left tiny goose bumps in its wake as her skin responded, tingling.

She wanted more.

Her nipples were already peaked, dark against the paleness of her breasts. She ached for his touch, knowing it would only increase the pulsing need between her legs. She was temped to take matters into her own hands, either draw his hands up to cover her breasts or play with her nipples herself. Another type of watching. But instead, she let him call the shots, explore as he wanted while he tracked the motions in the mirror before them.

He left trails of fire on her skin. Losing herself in a haze of pleasure, she was vaguely surprised that she couldn't see smoke rising, following the lazy patterns, as he slid along the waistband of her skirt, dipped into her navel, drew a line up between her breasts.

Finally, finally he cupped the globes in his hands, his thumbs stroking the heavy undersides. So close, a promise. He watched her expression, and she knew from his breathing that he saw her eyes had grown heavy-lidded with desire.

Her whole face showed it, in fact. Her lips, parted slightly as her own breathing increased. Her skin, flushed with excitement. Her hair, still tousled from their earlier walk on the beach.

She watched, fascinated, as he moved upward, grazed his palms over her sensitive nubs. Still, she wanted more, needed more. She shimmied her hips back against him, urging him on.

He took her nipples between his fingers, rolling them, kneading. The arousal flared higher, even faster than she expected, and she gasped. Swept away on the pleasure, she wasn't even aware that her eyes had fluttered shut until she heard his voice, thick with passion.

"Open your eyes, Callista."

She dragged them open. She looked drugged, and she was— drugged on pleasure so strong it bordered on pain. She'd had no idea she could reach such heights and still not come; could still ache, desperate to come, but at the same time want the delicious torture never to end.

If he continued tormenting her nipples like that, she might just come anyway.

The thought made her thighs weak. Her knees trembled from the strain of keeping her from collapsing to the floor in a puddle of need.

"Watch yourself," Evan continued. "Look how your body responds. Look at how you react."

He'd not only taken to this idea, he'd grabbed it with both hands and run with it. A fresh wave of moisture dampened her panties at the realization. He didn't need lessons, just suggestions. Once he had the basic concept, he had all the creativity and wicked imagination to build on it.

That turned her on more than she could have possibly imagined. She'd set free the tiger, and she had no idea how to tame it.

She didn't want to. She wanted to play with it, no matter what the risks. Danger was a delicious aphrodisiac.

Evan stopped the maddening manipulation of her breasts, but her nipples continued to throb even after his touch was gone. His hands were at her waistband now. He nudged her away from him so he could slide down the zipper of her skirt. When the garment landed at her feet, she kicked it away.

She stood before the mirror naked except for a scarlet silk thong and a pair of sling-back heels, flushed, aroused, trembling with desire.

Behind her, Evan put his hands on her shoulders and regarded her reflection as well. He was still mostly dressed, a fact that made her feel both vulnerable and powerful. His dark eyes took in her body, her expression.

He gazed down and shook his head. "Just a little excited, are we?" he asked.

She followed the line of his stare. A damp spot darkened the silk.

"You could…" She had to clear her throat. "You could find out just how much."

He chuckled. The sound sent a shiver down her spine.

"Oh, I fully intend to," he said, the words an erotic promise. "And you're going to watch me while I do."

His hand moved excruciatingly slowly down her belly until his fingertips rested at the elastic at the top of her thong. He slipped one finger under the edge. Then another. Inched his hand down, until his fingers cupped her mound, an inch above the core of her need. Her clit spasmed, silently begging for his touch.

Any touch.

"So hot," he whispered. "So steaming hot. I want to go down on my knees and lick you, but that would get in the way of watching, wouldn't it?"

She couldn't find the words to answer. All she could do was whimper at the thought of his tongue flicking against her clit.

Her inner muscles clenched.

He slipped his hand lower. His fingers slipped in her juices, toyed with her entrance. He stroked, a finger on either side of her clit. Barely touching. So close.

"Keep your eyes open," he growled.

It was almost impossible. The pressure built inside her, and she wanted nothing more than to throw her head back and give in to it. Forcing herself to focus seemed to delay her release, keep her poised on the knife edge, frantic to come but unable to reach the exact second of climax.

Thank god he had an arm wrapped around her waist, because she was sure she wasn't able to stand on her own anymore. He stroked her, inexorably bringing her higher and higher, until she thought she would die from the need.

"Watch yourself come," Evan said, and caressed her swollen clit.

She saw her mouth open, although she wasn't sure if she heard herself scream as the pleasure cracked her open; saw her hips jerk, thrusting herself against his fingers as she milked every last second of sensation from her body; saw the desire and satisfaction in his eyes.

He pressed his lips to her hair, held her against him while she gasped for air, regained equilibrium. Her heart's frantic tattoo calmed.

"Evan..."

She turned in his arms. His chest was hard against hers, and she felt it rise and fall with his breath. He brought his hand to his mouth, tasted her, and her body responded with another pulse, deep within her.

When she found the strength, she stripped his shirt the rest of the way off, then made short work of the rest of his clothes. When he was fully, gloriously naked in front of her, she sighed.

"Your turn," she said, and sank to her knees.

Using her hands, she urged his hips round so he stood sideways, their bodies in profile in the mirror. Evan grabbed the bedpost with one hand, bracing himself for the pleasure to come.

Callista smiled up at him, a promise.

His cock jutted out, proudly, a drop of moisture at its tip. Callista touched her tongue to it, flicking away the sweet bead. He sucked his breath in.

She darted her tongue out again, teasing. Touching here, there, blowing warm breath across him.

When she finally took him into her mouth, she tilted her head sideways, just a little, so she could see.

He was watching, fixated on the vision of her taking his hard length between her lips, sucking him in, swirling her tongue around the head before dipping deeper down. She used her hands sparingly, not wanting to get in the way of their view.

She was licking the underside of him when he finally groaned and drew her to her feet. He kissed her, a delicious bruising of her cock-swollen lips.

"I want to be inside of you," he said.

She found a condom in her purse, rolled it on him. He lay back on the bed, and she straddled him. She saw herself in the mirror before her, wild hair, lust-darkened eyes, orgasmic flush across her chest. Saw a wanton woman about to take her pleasure.

Evan put his hands on her hips, guiding her over him. The tip of him nestled between her lips, and she had the brief thought of teasing him, teasing them both. But she knew that they were both beyond teasing.

Splaying her hands on his chest, she eased herself down onto him, moaning with pleasure as he filled her.

No teasing. No waiting. She moved, dragging her hips up and down, impaling herself on him until she was thrusting back and forth, her desire peaking again.

He grabbed the headboard, letting her take control.

They both looked up, saw their reflection in the mirror above the bed: the muscles in his arms and chest taut, her head thrown back in ecstasy.

Their gaze met.

They came.

THE ROYALTON —A DARAY TALE

Tess Danesi

The first snowflakes have chosen today to make their appearance. I leave a trail of footprints in the thin layer of snow that tenaciously sticks to the sidewalk. For a short time, New York will be transformed into a clean and crisp wonderland. I walk a bit more briskly, snow crunching underfoot, careful not to slip in my high-heeled boots. I'm eager to get to the hotel. The doorman, shivering beneath his long black wool overcoat, greets me by name and holds the door open for me. Dar and I have made a habit of visiting the lounge at the Royalton. It's close to both our offices and prior to its recent renovation, was a quiet place to enjoy a cocktail in each other's company at the end of a long day. Now, the new décor has brought new crowds. Evenings after five, it's bustling with trendy New Yorkers, making us sometimes seek the smaller, cozier lounge at the Mansfield, with its library-like ambiance, when we desire less noise amid old world charm. I feel like Mata Hari at the Mansfield, ready to slide a microdot into Dar's waiting palm as we sip Manhattans.

"Stay warm, Tess," says Dean, my favorite doorman, with one final shudder.

"Thanks, you should take that advice yourself, Dean," I reply, wondering if he knows me well enough to sense my anxiety. More likely he thinks it's the cold making me tremble.

It's early; the crowds have not yet arrived, so I select a sofa in a corner, remove my camel cashmere coat, fold it, and place it next to me. I open my bag and remove the envelope Dar had delivered to my office. His instructions were simple.

> *Hello, pet. Be at the Royalton at four. Have one drink, charge it to room 1215. At 4:30 open the sealed envelope, and follow my numbered instructions.*

Like so many times before, I do what Dar requests, though I am tempted to rip open the envelope I now hold in my damp palm. My finger slides along the top edge, my palm presses against the flat surface, as if that will help me intuit what he's written inside. I've been twitchy with anticipation since noon when my assistant brought me the envelope and I read his brief message. I'm thankful that I wore a new dress and pretty new undies today, courtesy of the weekend's Christmas shopping spree. As the waitress brings me my usual Patron, chilled and strained into a frosted martini glass, I think how glad I am that Dar appreciates my near addiction to the accoutrements of femininity. Lace-topped thigh highs and delicate lacy undergarments make him wild. The first sip of the frosty liquid soothes my dry throat and I begin to relax. I know I won't finish my drink, I'm still too nervous, and with Dar it always pays to have my wits about me.

I look at my watch. *Damn the time. It just won't move.* I take another sip of my drink and stare at the envelope I have placed on the table in front of me. I feel the vein in my temple pulsate, indicating how tense I am. *He could simply be planning to take me to dinner*, I think in an effort to center myself. But I know it's more than that. I just wish I had some idea. Then again, I love Dar for many reasons, one of which is his constant ability to take me by surprise. Our relationship is tumultuous. No one has hurt me more, but at the same time, no one had ever made me feel more alive and more treasured than Dar. The price for his love is high; the bruises, more often present than not, on my ass and thighs are tangible manifestations of his sometimes sadistic excesses. But at the same time, no one has stood by me, loved me, and defended me with such vehemence. I often wonder at my ability to fear him and to trust him at the same time.

I glance at my watch and it holds me spellbound. I don't know why I wait for precisely four thirty to arrive. I guess I'm so used to following Dar's directives that I don't even consider how he'd never know if I jumped the gun by ten minutes. So I sit there taking the occasional sip of tequila and fixating on willing the thin silver hands to rotate. Finally, the time arrives and I slide a long cranberry lacquered fingernail under the flap, remove the sheet of Dar's cream-colored stationery, and read the first line. Written in his small, precise handwriting, the first sentence tells me to read and complete each instruction before going on to the next. I feel a familiar tingle between my thighs at the thought of what looks like a long and drawn out evening.

1) Use the enclosed card key and let yourself into room 1215.

I laugh to myself, thinking he should have penned a little stop sign, like those at the end of each section of standardized tests, after each line. It makes me smile as I head for the elevator. My gaiety is short-lived; the elevator goes directly to twelve and opens. I'm nervous as I make my way down the narrow hallway illuminated only by small sconces and glowing portholelike lights on each door. Room 1215 looms in front of me and with a mix of excitement and trepidation, I slide the card into the door, then hear a soft click before a pinpoint of green light announces that I may enter. The room has a cool elegance. It's sparsely though expensively furnished in cool tones of metallic gray and rich cream. Decadent linens cover the bed, which is made to look as though it belongs on a cruise ship and can be folded back into the wall. I have no baggage, only my coat and handbag, nothing to busy myself with. I hang up my coat, take the letter out of my bag, and place my purse on the closet shelf. I don't bother to sit before I read the next directive.

2) There's a bottle of Laphroaig on the credenza. Pour two tumblers and set them on the round glass table.

Two glasses of whiskey? My heart is thumping harder than ever. I put my hand on top of my breast, feeling the persistent rhythm against my palm and keeping it there until it slows. Dar knows one of my fantasies has been to be double penetrated by him and another man, but Dar, though he's had his share of kinky three- and more-somes with casual girlfriends, has never shared anyone he cared about deeply. As I pour the amber liquid into the two glasses, inhaling the heavy peaty aroma, I think how Dar has more than satisfied me sexually, awakening a deep and darkly masochistic side of my personality. While I am not submissive in general, I am submissive to him. In the midst of the tidal wave of passion and sadism that is Dar, I never gave much thought to actualizing this particular fantasy. And with Dar's jealousy, an emotion that has been known to stir up his profound capacity for cruelty, I worry that perhaps it would be best for all concerned to let it go unrealized. A threesome would explain why I am in this hotel room. This is something Dar would not want left to linger among the ghosts that haunt his home. It makes sense to do this here, in a place we can leave behind, abandoning any specters when we close the door behind us. I force myself to stop predicting, stop thinking, and look at the next line.

3) Strip to your bra and panties.

I quickly remove my dress and hang it up neatly in the closet, eager to get to the next instruction. Though I haven't read ahead, I've seen only a few more are left to go and then I'll be in Dar's arms. I can't wait. It may not be a warm embrace, I may be dealing with him in his cool and methodical mood, but to me just being in his presence is calming. Contradictions abound; with Dar I feel a deep inner peace even when I am at my most apprehensive. With Dar there are only extremes: I love him or I hate him, I feel safe or frightened; often I feel these emotions at the same time. What is a constant is my fathomless trust in him. I have a premonition I will be dipping into that well of faith tonight.

4) In the dresser drawer there is a blindfold and two sets of handcuffs. Bring them to the table. Sit in the middle seat.

I find the items just as he said; a thick black blindfold and two sets of steel handcuffs. My body feels as if it's vibrating, the way a kitten hums as it purrs contentedly in your arms, my cunt clenching as I hold the cold metal in my hands. I think how tight and unforgiving they'll feel wrapped around my wrists, and wonder if I'll be struggling so that they'll dig into and bruise my thin, delicate flesh. I sit down, my thighs feeling chilled against the frigid aluminum seat, realizing for the first time how cool the room is and knowing that Dar must have turned down the heat. My trembling excites him, be it from the cold or from uncertainty or from fear. I swallow hard, attempting to dislodge the lump in my throat, as I read his final instruction.

> 5) At 5:00, put on the blindfold, put a set of hand-cuffs around both wrists, and secure your left arm to the back rail of the chair. Wait.

He knows I hate this, that it's not safe to leave me restrained alone, that it will kick in my tendency to panic as my mind turns over all the horrific things that might happen, being in so vulnerable a position. Being in a hotel makes it worse, less predictable. Anyone could walk in. Being scared makes me wet; no one knows that better than Dar.

I know I don't have to do this but I also know that I will. The wetness soaking through my panties and glazing my inner thighs is evidence of how aroused I am despite my nerves. Looking at my watch, I see I only have five minutes to wait. With each minute, my anxiety escalates, and I'm not even restrained yet. I swallow hard against the lump in my throat and force myself to tear my eyes away from my watch. Whatever buzz I had from the drink is gone. Adrenaline flows through my body as I finally settle the blindfold over my eyes, making sure the handcuffs will be easy to reach once my sight is gone. The only noise in the room, the ratcheting sound of the cuffs tightening, competes with the sound of rushing blood in my head.

I don't wait long. Moments later, I hear a card slide into the door and the handle turns. "Hello, pet," he says simply. I reply in the same simple fashion, so nervous and agitated that even saying two words is a struggle. I listen hard to determine if there is anyone else in the room with him, but the thick carpet successfully muffles any sound. I jump when I feel his hand brush my cheek.

"Nervous, pet?" he queries.

"Yes, Dar," I whisper.

"Good," he replies. In my mind I can see the smirk on his handsome face. "You won't be seeing tonight, Tess, at least not until our guest leaves."

My free arm involuntarily covers my breasts at this confirmation that he isn't alone. I squeeze my thighs tightly together in an attempt to subdue the ache in my cunt. Nothing escapes his notice. He pulls my arm away and with a click of the metal sliding home I am utterly helpless.

"Excites you, doesn't it, my beautiful little bitch? Being so helpless, knowing we can do what we will with you?"

Oh, god—we. "Yes."

His breath is hot on my neck. Is it his breath, I suddenly wonder, as I feel him lock the other set of cuffs to the chair?

"I'm giving you what you want tonight, Tess. I'll be buried deep in your ass and another cock will be in that tight, hot cunt of yours. Of course, it will be my way, my rules. You will never know who it is touching you, whose cock you're gagging on. Does that suit you?"

I nod my head; my throat feels too dry to answer. Suddenly, warmth spreads through my face as his palm connects hard with my cheek.

"Answer me, bitch."

"Daray, please, please just tell me…" I start, beginning to panic at the thought that he might have invited a stranger. It disturbs me so much I use his full name to get his attention. I've always imagined this scene happening naturally, the result of an evening of comfortable companionship among friends and maybe a bit too much alcohol.

He reads my mind, he always does. How he does it I'll never know. I wish I could look into his eyes and see his thoughts with a modicum of the success he has at deciphering mine. As he leans into me, I picture him bending his long, muscular frame over the back of the chair as his rough cheek is pressed to my smooth, heated face. "Do you think I'd allow a stranger to touch you, pet? Tsk. Now be a good girl, no more questions."

"Have a seat," he says to the hushed presence.

Glasses clink as I picture them sitting there. Are they looking at me, appraising me? Are they ignoring me, content to sip their whiskey in silence? Time loses meaning and I begin to fidget in my seat. It might have been five minutes or twenty when I feel the chair being pushed back away from the table and strong hands roughly pull my breasts from my bra. I gasp and Dar quiets me. Warm liquid spills from my shoulders, over my breasts, down my belly and pools on the aluminum seat, mingling with the slick fluid that coats my sex and thighs. My senses are overwhelmed by the intense smoky aroma when a tongue starts to lick my neck slowly, so damn slowly, making its way down the gentle slope of my breast. My nipple is sucked into a hot mouth. Whose, I wonder? Then it doesn't matter as I feel the heat of another tongue following the same erotic path on the other side. My head rolls back as I revel in this decadent sensation. Teeth bite into one nipple, pulling and stretching it while the other mouth remains soft and supple on my breast. The conflicting sensations keep me even more on edge. I feel intoxicated as both tongues begin to move down my sides and lap up the liquid that has accumulated in the crease of my thighs. Teeth bite into the tender flesh of my inner thigh. The heat of a tongue pressed against the sheer scrap of fabric that barely covers my pussy makes me push myself greedily against whoever's mouth it is. I realize I don't care—I just don't want it to stop.

I lose the attention of one mouth as the handcuffs that restrain me are removed. I know the mouth that continues to press against my cunt isn't Dar's. Only Dar would have the keys. *Oh, god, oh, god*, I think, too lost in these moments to worry about Dar's reaction. Whatever will be will be as long as I continue to surrender myself to Dar and the moment. I'm pulled up from my seat, my bra removed, panties slid down my thighs until they puddle at my ankles.

"Step out," Dar says.

I do and I'm naked in front of my lover and this mysterious male presence. Given a moment to think, I wonder who this could be. I don't wonder for long. I'm pushed back onto the corner of the bed. Placed so that my cunt is available at one end and my head hangs off the other side. A cock is at my lips and I open eagerly to take it in. A male groan fills the room as it slides over my lips, into the velvety softness of my mouth, and down my throat. Hands spread my legs farther. I feel like a plaything, having no say in what gets done to me, a feeling I'm not sure I enjoy on a conscious level but here, now, while my clit is sucked into that mouth, pulled at, bitten, coaxed out of hiding, until it feels twice its normal size, and a rigid cock is fucking my face, there is no right and wrong, only pleasure. Sensations that carry me away until I feel myself slide over the edge and I'm bucking wildly against the face between my thighs, wanting to scream as I come but unable to because that cock is relentlessly pumping into my open mouth.

I want to know who is where but the silence of the men, except for grunts and moans, makes it impossible. Dar only talks when he wants me to know precisely where he is. I hope at one point he'll slip up but given his amazing level of self-control, I know that's unlikely. It seems the other man has taken a temporary vow of silence. Suddenly my mouth is empty; a hand surrounds my narrow wrist and pulls me into position.

I'm on top of someone. He lies flat underneath me and I think of letting my hands run down along his belly, wondering if that would give me an indication of who I am on top of. Before I can do anything, someone is behind me, his erect cock pressed against my ass. Hands are everywhere—alternately squeezing then slapping my breasts, spreading my ass. Fingers slide into my cunt and my ass, hands entwine in my hair. I'm floating yet grounded as the cock that is to claim my cunt impales me, taking my breath away for a moment. "Oh, fuck, oh, god, yes," I hear myself say and then I go silent as cool liquid is poured on and rubbed into my asshole.

"Relax, pet," Dar whispers into my ear. I'm comforted to know it's him behind me, his magnificent cock about to slide into my ass. Dar is big and thick, and the cock in my pussy now feels much the same; it fills me completely, making it hard to imagine it possible to have another cock inside me, even in another hole, at the same time.

The head of his cock prods my tight bud. He stops and takes a moment to use his fingers, adding more lube, stretching me slowly to prepare me. I almost cry; for Dar this is a display of tenderness. His breath warms my neck as he whispers more encouraging words in my ear. "Shhh, Tess, shhh," he says soothingly, even as the head of his cock pushes past my tense muscles, making me scream in an alien voice not mine, too feral to be coming from me. He takes a moment, kissing my neck, nuzzling my earlobes before pushing his entire length in. It's insanely intense; there are no words, what words would do? Only three rapidly beating hearts, three sweat-glazed bodies together in a primal bond, moaning and panting their pleasure as they move in rhythm.

As the movements get harder, more intense, Dar reverts to his

harsher self, pulling my hair so hard my neck hurts, biting pain-
fully into my shoulder, making me scream so loud for a moment
I worry about people in the next room or hallway hearing us.
His words are harsher as well. "Is this what you wanted, bitch?
You love it, don't you, my little whore? Can't get enough cock.
Is this enough for you? Is it?"

"Yes. Oh, god, yes," I shout. I'm surprised I can even speak
with the intensity of this new sensation. I can feel their cocks
touch through the thin wall separating my cunt from my ass. I
know they must feel each other too and it makes me even crazier.
I realize this must be someone Dar knows well and trusts implic-
itly. There is only one person I can think of who fits that bill, and
who is so similar in body type that it would be difficult to tell
them apart without my sight: Jack, his best friend, the bastard
who has always disliked me. Dar claims it's simply because Jack
is protective. I find it nearly impossible to believe that anyone
would think Dar needs protecting, but at the same time I am
begrudgingly grateful that Dar has so loyal a friend.

My thoughts vanish as they both pump harder into me. I'm
going to come, I can't help myself, it's too much, too intense, I
want it to continue forever, and I want it to stop immediately.
There is no more rhyme or reason to my thoughts. I'm crazed,
lost in a mad eddy of sensation and emotion when spasms rock
my body. My cunt tightens, strangling the heavy cock inside me,
my ass pulsating hard around Dar's cock. I hear a low groan,
and the hand stiffens in my hair; Dar pulls out of my ass and
roars as his come warms my back and flows, dripping in thick
rivulets, to coat my ass. He continues holding me, helping to lift
and lower me on the cock still enveloped inside me.

"Come again," he says in that voice that broaches no argu-
ment. "Come for me, slut. Come with that cock inside and my
hands on your throat."

When he moves his large hands to my throat, I inhale deeply, tightening every muscle in my body in anticipation of losing my breath for seconds that I know from experience will feel like hours. But he doesn't squeeze, he just presses firmly, allowing me my breath, though making me aware it's in his power to take it away as he pleases. My orgasm builds rapidly with the combination of his words, his firm hands, and the stiff cock pounding me hard enough to bump my cervix. As I come again I feel the man underneath me slam into me one final time. "Jesus fucking Christ," he exclaims. "Jesus Christ." I'm sure the words were unintentional but impossible to be restrained. Just those five words confirm that it is Jack. And as soon as I think that, I begin to doubt myself. At least I think it's him. I wonder if I'll ever be sure.

Dar lifts my limp body up and places me gently on the bed. I feel the bed shift as they both get up and then hushed whispers, words I can't make out. Water starts running in the bathroom. I want to get up and take off this damn blindfold, but I don't dare. I'm elated that Dar has made this fantasy come true for me. I know with his protectiveness and possessiveness, it couldn't have been easy for him. I wonder what, if any, price I'll have to pay. Then I laugh to myself, remembering one of Dar's rules—there is always a price to pay.

There are more whispers and finally the sound of the door opening and closing. The ghost has gone. I picture him vanishing, dissolving into mist before he even reaches the elevator, a phantom that will haunt the halls of this hotel forever. Dar tells me he's going to dim the lights. Then he walks to the bed, pulls me up to my knees, and slides the blindfold off. Even though the room isn't bright, I blink a few times as my eyes grow accustomed to sight. Then all I see are his deep brown eyes. I'm staring at him, trying to access his thoughts, his mood, when he smiles that devilish grin, halfway between a sneer and a smile. He's standing in front of me, naked, still with the glow of sex evident in the sheen on his body, his cock semierect.

"My trousers are on the chair. Go and bring me the belt from them, pet," he says. He doesn't take his eyes from mine until I walk past him on my way to do his bidding. "You can reimburse me with tears, Tess. I think that will do for now."

Ah, I think, a smile he can't see stretching across my face as I feel my own excitement start to build again, *that is a price I am more than willing to pay.*

SO SIMPLE A PLACE

Isabelle Gray

S erena stood out on the streets of Tokyo. With her exotic caramel complexion, long auburn corkscrew curls, and tall, slender frame, it was clear that she was *gaikokujin* but she didn't mind. Serena enjoyed being the center of attention. She was in Japan for six months overseeing a corporate merger and three months in she had learned several things, not the least of which was that she had eaten enough seafood to last a lifetime, it was indeed possible to survive on ramen, and she was in desperate need of a lover. Serena had been on a few casual dates, mostly with expat Americans with a taste for *exotic* women—men who were simply *fascinated* about her experiences as a black woman in Japan—long on dull conversation and short on charisma or chemistry. While Serena enjoyed being the center of attention, she was less enamored with serving as an object of attention. And so, after awkward good-byes and empty promises of future encounters, these men were quickly forgotten. Most nights, she ended up in her king-sized bed with her favorite vibrator, the one thing that followed her around the world from client to client. But then there was Daichi Sato, her Japanese counterpart with whom she had been engaged in an elaborate, intoxicating flirtation.

Serena spoke little Japanese. Daichi spoke little English. And so they settled on French as their *lingua franca*. For three months, they had shared lunch each day in the small cafeteria, sitting across from one another, their fingertips almost touching as they enjoyed one another's company. Serena learned that Daichi had attended college in Montreal and loved everything about Canada. She knew that he lived with family, was single, loved hamburgers, listened to music whenever he could, and had only started liking his job when she had arrived on the scene. Daichi learned that Serena also loved music, had always moved around as an Army brat, and went to law school because she loved to argue. He knew that she enjoyed her work, craved the anonymity of never staying in one place for long, and had finely honed an ability to leave things behind.

One afternoon, after a particularly intense conversation, in which Serena confessed her loneliness, Daichi left her a text message asking her to meet him in the hall near the bathroom. As they made their way to the last stall, her stiletto heels echoed against the floor tiles. Serena glanced at their reflections from the corner of her eye—her tall figure, and Daichi's compact, muscular frame. She liked the contrast. She entered the stall first. It was just wide enough—clean in the manner of most Japanese bathrooms—and smelled faintly of antiseptic cleanser. Serena wore a charcoal pencil skirt that stopped a few inches above her knees, a wide red belt, and a tight French blue blouse open at the collar. She loved dressing up for work—for Daichi if she was honest about it—carefully choosing seductive yet tasteful outfits that catered to active imaginations. Daichi leaned forward, traced the line of her chin, and placed a moist kiss at the pulse point at the base of Serena's throat.

"I've been wanting to do that since the first time I saw you," he murmured.

Serena shivered and leaned back. Daichi drew his lips upward until he found Serena's mouth, and shyly pressed his lips to hers, wrapping his arms around her waist. As the warmth of his body seeped into hers, Serena parted her lips, tapping her tongue ring against Daichi's tongue.

"And I've been wanting to do that," she said.

Daichi's hand slid firmly up her back and into her hair, his fingers tangling in the wild mess of long curls. Their tongues met almost gracefully and Serena imagined the moment as a postcard she would save for herself. Her thighs tingling, Serena hooked a foot around Daichi's calf, pulling him closer. Suddenly they both tensed, as a door opened, and then there was a rush of water. Daichi pressed a finger against Serena's lips and grinned. With his other hand, he slowly inched her skirt up around her hips and slipped his fingers beneath the waistband of her panties, where Serena was hot and wet. She nipped at his finger with her teeth, spreading her legs slightly. Deftly, Daichi began stroking Serena's clit, so softly it almost hurt. Her breath quickened and she gripped Daichi's shoulders to brace herself, urging him to stroke harder. The person who had entered began humming as he dried his hands. Daichi rubbed Serena's clit harder, kissing the exposed expanse of her cleavage, then quietly, he whispered in halting English, so only she could hear, "Do you like?"

Serena nodded, rapidly, her eyelids fluttering. She reached down, covered Daichi's hand with hers, and gently grazed her fingernails across his almond skin. Daichi nodded and slid two fingers inside Serena's pussy, enjoying the tight sensation of her membranes taking hold. As they heard the door open and they were once again alone, Serena gasped aloud.

"I can't believe we're doing this," she said, gripping his shoulders.

Daichi thrust his fingers until they were deeply buried. "It is a very productive use of our time."

Again, Serena nodded, leaning down to kiss Daichi hungrily, their tongues and teeth colliding sloppily with quiet chaos. Daichi twisted his hand so he could stroke her clit with his thumb as he slid his fingers in and out of her pussy, faster and faster, until Serena slammed her head back against the stall and allowed herself a loud moan. The orgasm quickly spiraled through her body, leaving her legs weak and rubbery. As they emerged from the stall, Daichi blew on his wet fingers and straightened his tie. Serena pulled her skirt back down and ran her fingers through her hair, eyeing her flushed complexion in the mirror.

"Do I look okay?" she asked.

Daichi smiled at her in the mirror, and helped Serena adjust her blouse. "You look stunning."

Later, in a meeting, surrounded by their colleagues, Daichi slowly dragged his fingers under his nose and discreetly blew Serena a kiss. *This is nowhere near as productive,* he wrote in a text message as he held his BlackBerry beneath the conference table.

For the next several weeks, they continued their harried bathroom encounters, driving each other into satisfying frenzies but never fully consummating the relationship. When they passed each other in the halls, Daichi reached for her fingers or quickly looked around and gently squeezed her ass. When they were joined by colleagues for lunch, they would sit side by side and Serena would rest her hand on Daichi's thigh, squeezing Daichi's cock at well-chosen moments. They shared secret smiles whenever they exchanged glances. Stitching these stolen moments together, they created a tiny universe where the rest of the world didn't matter—where they were more alike than different. It had been enough until it wasn't, Serena thought as they sat in yet another meeting listening to the other lawyers run through the finer points of corporate mergers.

You have a gift for foreign tongues, Serena texted Daichi as she grinned at him across the wide mahogany conference table and slowly uncrossed her legs, leaned forward, and exposed her cleavage just enough to make Daichi twitch. After taking a sip of water, she leaned back, tossing her hair over her shoulder.

Busy tonight? Daichi wrote back. Serena looked up and shook her head. *Then tonight, I shall show you my Tokyo.*

Serena's stomach fluttered. Most evenings were spent in the hotel where she shared a two-bedroom suite with Dean Preston III, an American colleague who, from what she could hear through the thin walls of the suite, spent his nights working his way through the female population of Japan, one or two women at a time. The only parts of Tokyo she had seen were those places between work, the hotel, and the hotel gym and bar. Many nights were spent watching Japanese game shows, American shows dubbed in Japanese, or working out in the gym that overlooked the city. From the elliptical, she admired the never-ending traffic and bright lights flashing below, but never quite mustered the energy to actually explore what was beneath those lights for herself. A lot, she realized, was lost in translation.

For the rest of the day, she distracted herself from mundane corporate details by wondering where Daichi would take her. A little after seven, when she had finished for the day and was packing up her briefcase for the night, Daichi approached her from behind, resting a gentle hand in the small of her back. It was a confident, possessive gesture that turned Serena on. She closed her eyes and inhaled deeply.

"Are you ready?" he asked.

Serena snapped her briefcase shut and turned around. Throwing caution to the wind, she traced Daichi's lips with her thumb. "I am."

He wrapped his long fingers around her wrist and kissed the palm of her hand. "Let me take that," he said, reaching for the briefcase.

"Are you always this polite?"

"It's all about context."

"That's good to know," Serena said, grinning.

When they exited their building, it was already dark and the street was bustling with evening traffic. Serena hooked her arm beneath Daichi's and they walked several blocks to a small, nondescript restaurant with no visible sign. Inwardly, Serena groaned. She was not up to another adventure in Japanese cuisine. Daichi noticed her grimace.

"Don't worry," he said, with his easy smile and a wink. "This place serves the best American food in Tokyo."

Inside, the décor reminded Serena of a lonely highway diner. Against the far wall stood a long counter with four red stools, and the rest of the small restaurant was filled with matching booths. A Billy Joel song played on the stereo and they could hear the sound of dishes being washed in the kitchen. A family with two young children sat in one booth, and an old man ate alone at the counter. The rest of the restaurant was empty, save for two waitresses. As they sat, Serena breathed a sigh of relief, reaching for a plastic menu, one side in English, the other in Japanese.

"I thought you might be craving a taste of home," Daichi said.

Serena eyed Daichi over the top of the menu. "I'm craving all sorts of things."

Daichi looked away, reddening slightly. Beneath the table, Serena slid her foot out of her patent leather platform heel and dragged her toes, wiggling them slightly, up Daichi's calf and between his thighs, stopping when her foot was only inches away from his cock. When Daichi tried to slide forward, Serena pulled her foot away.

"What do you have a taste for?" she asked.

Daichi made an elaborate show of studying the menu for a few moments. "I can't seem to find what I'm looking for here."

Serena slid her foot forward until it was pressed firmly against Daichi's cock, which shifted noticeably in response. "Maybe we should get out of here."

Daichi nodded eagerly. After weeks of anticipation, they were both ready to take their relationship to a more intimate level.

"Should we go back to your place?" Serena asked, winking.

There was an awkward silence. Daichi stared at his hands and shifted uncomfortably in his seat. "Can we go to your hotel?"

Serena shook her head. "I have a roommate, remember? Don't tell me you have a wife at home."

Daichi blushed harder, the flush of red creeping down his neck. "I live with my parents and grandparents. It wouldn't be... possible for us to go there. They wouldn't approve."

"I don't get to meet the family?"

Daichi thought for a moment, struggling to find the right words. "It isn't that I don't want you to. It's that they would not understand why I had brought you home."

Serena set the menu on the table, trying to quell mild irritation. "Maybe I should just go back to my hotel. I wouldn't want you to do anything your family wouldn't approve of."

As she stood up, Daichi quickly looked around and grabbed her hand. Serena's pulse quickened again. "It's not like that," he said softly.

Serena sat back down. "What is it like?"

"We are a very insular culture. We are...traditional."

"You don't seem beholden to tradition when I am on my knees," Serena said sharply.

Daichi stood, holding his hand out. "I couldn't care less about tradition. I know a place we can go—where things will be a little simpler."

With his hand at the small of her back again, Daichi steered Serena onto the street. He hailed a cab and after telling the driver where he wanted to go, he and she sat silently, their thighs touching, Daichi's hand resting on Serena's knee. As the cab slowed, Serena moved to the window and stared up at a brightly lit hotel with a large, orange neon sign on the roof that read GLOBE HOTEL, and in smaller print just beneath, AROUND THE WORLD IN 80 SUITES.

Serena arched an eyebrow. "This is different."

Daichi grinned, raised his eyebrows, and handed the driver several bills. "This is a more interesting place in my Japan."

Inside the lobby, they were greeted with a small open space, and on the wall opposite the door, a large panel, resembling a vending machine interface with Japanese *kanji* and pictures that served as buttons. Another couple, an older man with a much younger woman, her face garishly painted with makeup, were also looking at the available selections, holding hands, and giggling as they decided between a night in Brazil or a tryst in Greece.

"This is a love hotel. It's where couples like us can come to enjoy one another."

Serena carefully studied the images before her. "How does this work?"

"If a picture is lit, the room is available. The world is at your fingertips, so to speak. You can stay for a rest or overnight. I put my credit card in this slot," Daichi said, pointing to the left. "Then we get a receipt and a key from the slot over there," he said, pointing to a small window near the elevators.

"How efficient," Serena said dryly.

"You're mad at me?"

Serena crossed her arms across her chest. "I don't know what I am."

"Stay the night with me?" Daichi asked. "I am nothing like my family. I think very highly of you and nothing could ever change that."

Serena looked around the small lobby, decorated with artifacts from around the world and two fake palm trees standing guard near the entrance. Then she looked at Daichi, his honest eyes, his tender smile, his confident hands, and suddenly a little thing like tradition no longer seemed important.

"I'd like that," she said.

"Where will we go tonight? There are many places in the world where tradition doesn't matter," Daichi said, tapping his chest just above his heart.

Serena relaxed and leaned against Daichi, her chin perched on his shoulder. She flicked her tongue against his earlobe and blew lightly. "I've always wanted to visit Rome," she mused.

Daichi pressed the picture of Rome and the panel chirped. He paid fifteen thousand yen and just as quickly, Serena heard a rush of air. The small window next to the elevator rose and inside was a small canister holding a receipt and a room key. They stood on opposite ends of the elevator, Serena undoing the top two buttons of her blouse as she watched Daichi watching her. When the doors opened, Daichi extended his arm. "After you," he said. "I'm sure you've heard this before, but I like to watch you walking away." Serena smiled to herself and put an extra strut in her walk as she led the way to their room.

They walked down a long hallway, hearing an intriguing range of sounds emanating from many of the rooms. Once inside their room, Serena pushed Daichi against the door, holding his arms over his head, entwining her fingers with his. She kissed Daichi wetly, a subtle warmth weaving its way through her body. Daichi pulled their arms down to their sides, holding Serena's hands behind her back, pushing her toward a large, round bed in the middle of the room. As she stepped backward, Serena kicked off her heels and laughed as she took in the room's décor for the first time. The walls were adorned with ornate Italian murals and along one wall stood several marble statues. The ceilings were lined with square mirrors and at the end of the bed was a large flat-screen television. Daichi pushed Serena onto the bed and tore off his shirt, several buttons flying. Serena reached for his belt, helping her lover out of his pants, groaning loudly as he knelt over her, one of his muscular thighs between hers, his knee pressed against her cunt.

She crawled higher, perching herself against a high stack of embroidered pillows.

Daichi slid the tip of his cock inside Serena's pussy, but she planted a hand firmly against his chest and pushed him away.

"Wait. I want to make myself wet for you," she said, throatily. She did, after all, enjoy being the center of attention.

Serena shimmied out of her clothes and lay before Daichi completely naked. Pulling her legs up, she spread herself wide and sucked on her middle finger, wetting it completely, before drawing a trail of saliva down the center of her body. With the palm of her hand splayed over her mound, which was covered in a dark pelt of neatly trimmed hair, she pressed her middle finger against her clit, hissing lightly as she found a pleasurable groove by stroking herself harder and harder until she felt herself on the edge of coming, then stroking lightly until her body ached for more. Daichi propped himself on one elbow at the foot of the bed, watching Serena intently, his erect cock jutting outside of his wool slacks.

"Do you like what you see?" Serena asked as she slid her fingers between her swollen pussy lips, then slid her finger into Daichi's mouth. He lapped her finger eagerly, then grabbed it with his teeth, twisting his head from side to side. He moaned softly, enjoying her not quite bitter taste. As Serena sank deeper into the pillows behind her, Daichi knelt between her thighs, sliding his hands from her knees to her waist, then up along her torso. He moved slowly, trying to memorize her body's contours with his own skin. Serena wrapped her legs around Daichi's waist, locking her ankles against his back. She pulled his neck to her mouth and sank her teeth into his skin, sucking softly. Daichi carefully inched his cock inside Serena until she was completely filled. Looking into Serena's eyes, he caressed her cheek, pulled back, and thrust his hips, harder this time.

"Yes," Serena gasped, lifting her hips to meet each thrust.

Daichi continued rocking his hips, sliding his open hand down Serena's face, squeezing her soft, full breasts between his fingers, pulling at her nipples with his teeth until they stretched taut.

"Harder. Fuck me harder," Serena muttered through clenched teeth.

Daichi planted his hands on either side of Serena's shoulders and, arching his back, thrust his cock harder, reaching for the deepest, tightest parts of Serena's cunt.

As she rose to meet him, Serena reveled in the sound of their bodies slapping together and coming apart. Moving against one another, they silently told each other all the things that had gone unsaid. She clawed at Daichi's slick back with her fingernails, leaving angry red trails on his flesh, and he growled hoarsely.

Daichi reached behind his back, pulling her ankles apart, spreading Serena's thighs until her ankles hung over the edges of the bed and her straining muscles quivered.

"I want you spread wide for me," he said.

Serena threw her head back, covering her mouth. She screamed into her hand and felt a hot rush of wetness between her thighs. Spread open this way, the sensation of Daichi's cock sliding in and out of her cunt only intensified, bringing her to the fine line between pain and pleasure over and over again. She looked up at their reflections in the mirrors—Daichi's powerful frame covering hers, the contrast of their bodies. What started as a light vibration just beneath her navel traveled lower, to her throbbing clit. Serena reached between their bodies, pressing her fingers so hard against her clit she felt the hard bone beneath. When she came, it was a sharp stab of sensation that ran through her entire body and left her breathless.

Serena's cunt gripped him tighter and Daichi began fucking her faster, almost furiously, his hips jerking uncontrollably. Just as he was about to come, he withdrew, leaving Serena curiously cold and empty. His cock spasmed, shooting thick silver strands across Serena's stomach, her body shuddering in response. His chest heaving, Daichi collapsed alongside her, massaging his come into her skin.

Afterward, as Daichi lay sprawled on the bed half asleep, Serena began to explore the room. In the bathroom, she found beautiful marble floors and a lovely fountain that emptied into a Jacuzzi tub. In the far corner of the room, a leather sling hung from four hooks. On one nightstand were three small bottles of lube, an assortment of condoms in a crystal vase, a bottle of massage oil, a remote control, and a copy of the *Kama Sutra*. On the other, she found a leather-bound folder and, jumping back onto the bed, she kissed Daichi's shoulder and shook him awake.

"What's this?"

Daichi rubbed his eyes, sitting up slowly, his cock still hard despite their earlier exertions. "That is like a room service menu. You can order food, drink…adult accessories."

Serena arched an eyebrow and stretched herself along Daichi's body, tracing his calf with her toes. "What kind of accessories?"

He began feathering his thumb across her nipple, then gently twisting it between his forefinger and thumb. "Most anything you can imagine."

"You should order us something," Serena said, sliding one leg over Daichi's, pressing her wet cunt against his thigh.

Daichi reached for the phone, dialed 0, and said a few hurried phrases in Japanese, of which Serena only understood every three words. Twenty minutes later, there was a soft knock at the door. Daichi wrapped a towel around his waist, and when he opened the door, a small cart covered with a white cloth was waiting. Chuckling to himself, he pulled the cart into the room.

"You seem to know a lot about these love hotels of yours," Serena observed. "You must bring many women here."

"Not as many as you might think. And no one that has mattered until recently."

Serena slid to the edge of the bed, resting her cheek against Daichi's stomach as she wrapped her hand around his cock, rubbing her thumb back and forth across the sensitive tip. "I bet you say that to all the girls."

Daichi ran his fingers through Serena's thick hair with one hand, while lifting the cloth from the cart with the other, revealing a freshly uncorked bottle of champagne, a platter of raw oysters, and a new package of red anal beads. "Something for me, something for you, something for us," he said.

"Which is which?"

Daichi raised an oyster shell above his mouth, letting the cool meat slide into his throat, but didn't answer. After tossing the empty shell onto the cart, he took hold of Serena's waist, turning her around so she faced away from him. With his cock pressed between her asscheeks, rocking back and forth, he kissed the back of her neck, and began moving his lips along her spine until he reached the small of her back. Serena crawled back onto the bed, resting on her arms and knees, her forehead on the mattress. She looked back over her shoulder, shivering as Daichi held the bottle of champagne high in the air, letting the amber liquid rain onto her and gather in the small of her back. Dragging his lower lip from her ass upward, Daichi began catching drops of champagne with his tongue. Serena giggled nervously, clenching her asscheeks. Daichi smacked her ass lightly, reached for a bottle of lube, and squeezed a healthy dollop between Serena's asscheeks.

"I've never done anything like this before," Serena said.

Daichi began massaging Serena's asshole in a slow circular motion. "You're in good hands."

Serena flexed her toes, spreading her legs as wide as she could, her ass high in the air.

Daichi draped the string of anal beads, eight in all, across Serena's lower back.

"Just remember to breathe."

Serena closed her eyes and inhaled deeply. As she exhaled, Daichi slid the first bead into her ass, pressing it forward until he felt a pop. Serena winced, forced herself to breathe steadily, and slowly relaxed as her muscles accommodated the change in density. Daichi inserted a second bead, then massaged her with more lube. As her ass stretched to accommodate all eight beads, Serena found herself more turned on than she had ever been, her pussy so wet she could smell herself. Daichi ate another oyster, then held the champagne bottle to Serena's lips. She drank hungrily, and as the champagne coursed through her body, she felt decadent and light-headed. Serena started gyrating her hips in a circle, desperate to grind her clit against the bed, a pillow, anything. Daichi held her still. "Don't move. Just breathe."

Serena groaned in frustration. "I want you to fill all of me," she said.

Daichi wrapped his fingers in Serena's hair and pulled her lips to his, bruising her with his mouth, forcing his tongue into her, swallowing the very breath from her body. Holding her against him, her back pressed to his chest, he buried his cock in her tender pussy. She gasped, pulling away and rearing back as her body readjusted to his girth. The beads shifted in her ass, sending curious waves of pleasure down Serena's legs. Daichi wrapped an arm around her body, clasping her throat with his hand.

Serena struggled for air, trying to balance her body against his. Sliding his hand up her neck with her own, she sucked two of his fingers and two of hers into her mouth, making loud sloppy noises. Daichi closed his eyes, trying to stay in control, but Serena began moving her hips in fast, wide circles, his cock touching every inch of her pussy. Daichi held Serena tighter still. In the mirror, their bodies looked like one.

"I'm going to come again," Serena moaned.

"Come for me."

"Only for you," Serena said.

As her body trembled, Daichi held her steady, and taking hold of the string for the anal beads, he pulled them out of her ass in one swift motion. Serena's mouth flew open but no sound came out. An intense wave of pleasure rolled through her body and tears began streaming down her face. She curled into a small ball in the center of the bed, shivering uncontrollably. His cock still inside her, Daichi wrapped his body around hers, and they fell asleep sweaty, spent, entwined.

In the morning, on the sidewalk in front of the hotel, they stood, foreheads pressed together.

"In my Japan, we only say *aishiteru* if we are so overwhelmed by emotion that we cannot contain it. We aren't as open with expressing our feelings as perhaps other people are."

"*Aishiteru,*" Serena said. "What does it mean?"

"It means I love you."

Serena nodded slowly. "*Aishiteru,*" she whispered. "Too bad the world isn't so simple a place as the heart."

Daichi kissed Serena softly. "The world is only as complicated as we make it."

Serena smiled. "Where will we go tonight?"

Daichi took her hand and they began walking. "Anywhere in the world," he said.

HEART-SHAPED HOLES

Madlyn March

A little to the right," John said.

I moved to the right.

"Now do that thing," he commanded.

"What thing?"

"You *know*. That *thing*. You did it like five minutes ago."

All of a sudden, I remembered: I moved my knees as far apart as they would go and lifted my arms straight up in the air. Well, at least all those years of gymnastics were finally coming in handy.

"Yeah, just like that," he said.

God, this was humiliating. A wife was supposed to give her husband pleasure on his wedding night, not help him get better reception of two *other* people going at it. Yes, that's right. I was barely three hours into my marriage and already a failure at fucking. I'd graduated with a 4.0 from Harvard but was unable to pull off what even the dumbest pigeon can do. I deserved this punishment, I thought, as I attempted a move that would make the most skilled modern dancer jealous. There. Now John could more clearly see Lola licking the naughty go-go dancer's behind. I confess that it was a bit of a shock finding out John liked this stuff. He was a good Christian, after all. But I suppose God and lesbian porn are not mutually exclusive interests.

I sighed. Nothing was turning out the way I'd dreamed it would. Since the day John had proposed, I'd thought of my wedding night. I'd relax on the softest pillow and he'd plunge into me like I was the softest pillow. But in reality, the pillows felt like bricks and I was tighter than your average J.Lo dress.

We'd go to Doctor Mathers next week, John promised. Doctor Mathers would know what was wrong. Doctor Mathers had probably seen this before. Doctor Mathers, patron saint of hymenally challenged wives everywhere.

After we tried to fuck, I sat on the bed and cried. I wasn't just crying from the pain, though. What bothered me was that John didn't even try to help. I had read in a number of books the many ways a man could make sex easier for a woman, but John had done none of those things. He just made me feel like a freak who needed medical attention.

But I was trying not to let that bother me. Maybe he'd be more patient one day, I thought hopefully. Maybe the sex would get better. And if it didn't, I still wouldn't divorce him. It was just sex, after all. I didn't even know what it felt like. Maybe sexual fulfillment for a woman was just something somebody made up, like Santa Claus or the Easter Bunny. Anyway, we'd been happy before, so why should this make a difference? I was sure I'd eventually get used to his penis inside me. If I got lucky, maybe I'd get him to masturbate me or go down on me. Anyway, the companionship was what was important. That was what lasted when you were eighty, not the fucking.

I watched John again.

"Bloody fuck," he cried out. "Look at them kissing."

I stared at the objects of his affection. I wondered what that would feel like—a pair of soft lips against my own. John's were always so chapped.

Then I started to get depressed again. I began thinking about heart-shaped holes. I realized there were two in our room at that moment. One in the bathroom—that huge, Valentine-shaped Jacuzzi—and the other in my chest. That Jacuzzi should have been filled with water and bubbles and John and me. My heart should have been filled with passion. But both were empty.

John continued to masturbate, not noticing my emotional distress. I looked away from him, embarrassed, but then curiosity got the better of me. I'd never seen a man touch himself before. Something was happening. Something huge. You could sense it in the air.

And then, all of a sudden, he began to growl, louder than the MGM lion. A spurt of liquid hit the wall.

I made a mental note to tip the chambermaid well.

After he came, he fell asleep. I carefully got out of my pose, not wanting to disturb him. I shut off the TV and decided to get some ice from down the hall. My pussy was still throbbing something fierce.

A woman was already at the machine.

"Ugh," she said, kicking it. "Damn thing's not working. Again." I detected a slight Southern accent.

"I guess your husband won't enjoy his beer, then," I said, pointing to her six-pack.

"No, cause a: I ain't got one, and b: even if I did, I wouldn't let him anywhere near my liquor. I'm Maxie, by the way." She stuck out her hand. I shook it, not knowing what else to do.

"You're here all by yourself?" I asked.

"Yep. Just like the Eric Carmen song. You know?" She started singing, but I put up a hand. I don't suffer the tone deaf gladly.

"I've heard it before," I said.

"Well, I am very much by myself right now," she said. "My girl—My partner left me. I'm still trying to recover." She put a hand through her short dark hair and sighed loudly.

So, she was a lesbian. Huh. Looked nothing like those women John was watching on TV. She was tougher, more masculine, but pretty in her own way.

"I just got married," I offered.

"Well then, guess I won't tell you all my theories about the foolishness of romance." She laughed. "But if it works out, you're damn lucky. Like I said, I miss it."

I didn't tell her I felt just as lonely as she did.

"Aren't you afraid to be here alone?" I asked, and silently cursed John for being so cheap. Another hundred and we could have been in a place without prostitutes patrolling the lobby. The folks at Lovers' Paradise conveniently forgot to mention that little amenity in their ad copy.

"No," she said. "I'm not afraid. I can handle myself. I'm used to it. I travel alone all the time. I'm a saleswoman. I'm here for the convention."

"Convention?" I asked.

"For the sex toys."

I blushed instantly.

"I'm sorry. I usually don't just come out with it like that. Must be this," she said, hitting a beer can. "I had one or two in the room before I came out here." She smiled. "Lowers my inhibitions."

She was making me uncomfortable. She stared at me for a few minutes. I stared at my feet.

"Well, I should go," I said.

"Oh, yeah, sure," she said, looking a little disappointed. "Congratulations, by the way."

"On what?"

"On what, she asks. You just got married, silly."

"Oh, right."

"You don't sound too happy."

"No, I am. It's just—It's complicated." *And something I'm not going to discuss with an intoxicated woman who peddles fake penises for a living.*

"Well, if you ever feel like talking about it, my door is always open," she said, smiling. "I have a degree in psychology. I don't use it for much nowadays, but I like to play armchair Dr. Phil occasionally." She stared at me. "You okay?"

I stared at the ceiling, trying not to cry. *This is not where I should be,* I thought. *I should be back in my hotel room screwing my husband's brains out, not in a dusty, dirty hallway making conversation with some perverted saleswoman.*

"Look, come to my room," she said.

"I can't. I have to get back. My husband—"

"Your husband won't miss you for a few minutes. Come now. I won't bite. I gave that up years ago," she said, winking.

John, I silently screamed. *Come out here and rescue me. Properly make me a woman. Or just talk to me.* But John was sleeping. I would be awake all night, playing the scenes of my terrible first time over and over in my head. I didn't want to be alone. So I followed her.

"What's your name?" she asked.

"Elizabeth," I said.

"Like the queen."

"Yeah, but I'm not nearly as elegant."

"Oh, you're elegant enough," she said.

When I got to her room, I saw it was the same layout as mine, including the heart-shaped tub.

"Tacky, right?" she said. "But it's kind of fun to splash around in."

"I haven't used mine yet," I admitted.

"Oh, you've got to. It has the best feature. Streams of hot water come shooting out of these jets and if you position yourself right on one, you can have the orgasm of your life."

I turned red.

"Oh, I'm making you feel embarrassed again. Can't shut my damn trap sometimes. I apologize. Have a beer."

I smiled and took one. "You're talking to the wrong person about sex. I can't have any kind of orgasm. I'm frigid. That's why I got so upset before. My husband and I—This was our first night and I couldn't—" I started crying again.

"Oh, no, honey. No," she said, rubbing my shoulder. "It's not your fault. He probably just doesn't know what to do. Men don't always know—"

"No, I can't have sex. It's as simple as that. I'm a freak."

"I am sure you are *not* a freak. How long have you been together?"

"A few months."

"Do you have a lot in common?"

Did we? It occurred to me right then that I didn't know. Oh, god. What the hell had I gotten myself into?

"Do you enjoy being close to him? The hugging, the kissing?"

"I hate kissing."

"You do?"

"Yes. Always have."

"Hmm," she said, touching her thumb thoughtfully to her chin.

"Well, I mean my husband's the only one I've ever kissed. His lips are kind of chapped; maybe that's it. We were—Well, he was watching this porn film. God, I can't believe I'm telling you this. I guess this lowers my inhibitions too," I said, pointing to the can.

"Anyway," I continued, "we were watching this lesbian porn film, and I thought maybe a woman's lips, just that they're softer, not that I'm a lesbian or anything. Not that there's something wrong with it, but I'm not. So this woman's lips, I thought, like, if I could get inside the TV and...okay, I'm not making much sense now, am I?"

"That's fine. Sense is highly overrated. But forget about that for a second. I have an exciting experiment in mind for you."

"What is it?" I asked, thinking maybe she had some kind of magical potion that could make me come with my husband.

"Get in the tub. Position yourself against one of the jets. If you can't get off that way, then you'll know you have a problem. But if you can, then you'll know *he's* the problem." She smiled. "Just sit in there for a little while, and when you're done, let me know what you think."

I sat outside the tub for a long time, wondering what to do. This weird woman was telling me to have an orgasm in her room. Of all the things I thought would be happening on my wedding night, this was not one of them. But none of the things I had thought would be happening on my wedding night were happening anyway. What the hell? I was here. Nobody would ever know. And I was curious.

I undressed, turned the water on, and went in. I searched for a jet. I found it and slowly pushed my pussy up to it. At first, it was just a pleasant feeling, like when you get a massage. But then the pressure felt different, and I got a very strange urge to thrust my hips against the water like a maniac. The pain in my pussy was now definitely forgotten.

The more I pushed myself up to the flow, the more intense the feeling was. All I wanted to do was sit there all day with water gushing between my legs. And yet I was going mad. This was nice, but there had to be something more. I was desperate for some resolving of this torture, but there was no relief, only more excitement.

And then the water shut off.

My heart was pounding wildly. It took me a few minutes to regain my breath.

It took me a few more to realize I was not alone.

"Still think you're a freak?" Maxie asked, standing over me.

"Why are you here?" I asked. I knew it was rude but I was so wound up, I couldn't be polite.

"I wanted to see how you were doing. You're doing well. Showed that jet a good time."

"You were watching me?"

She nodded.

"But—but—" I was livid. How dare she do that!

"Relax. I'm a trained professional."

"Very funny. And why did you shut it off like that? I was just about to—"

"Come like a madwoman? I know. But I wanted to show you that you can get off with human contact as well."

"I'm not a les—I mean, I told you already. I'm married."

"*Just* married. And it doesn't seem like that's working out so well for you, as Dr. Phil might say."

I stood up, without realizing for a second that I was naked. "You don't know John!" I yelled. "He's a wonderful man."

"Yeah," she said. "So wonderful he can't even get his wife off on her wedding night. So wonderful she's fantasizing about kissing a woman in a porno." She looked at me closely.

"God, you have the most amazing tits," she said.

"You have no right—"

"Oh, please. Get off your high horse, Dale Evans. I'm here to help you."

"Are you kidding? How is this helping?"

"I *was* you about ten years ago. Thought I was straight, did the whole marrying thing. Had no clue why I couldn't come that night. Or any night after, for that matter. Didn't know why until a good friend of mine showed me what I was missing."

"I'm not—"

"The same as I was? No, you're not. You're still in that hopeful state. You still think the marriage will get better. You think those fantasies you have about other women are normal, something every straight woman has. Well, my dear. I'm here to inform you they aren't."

"I'm leaving," I said. Served me right. What did I think I was doing, going off with some stranger like this? I had to go back to my room, go back to John.

But before I could get my clothes on, she pushed me against the wall. I struggled, frightened. I had rejected her advances. Who knew how she'd react?

Then, all of a sudden, I knew. She reached down to my clit and began rubbing. "You're so horny," she whispered. "You need release. All that pent-up pleasure. It has to be brought out or you'll go insane. And who's going to bring it out, huh?" she asked, kissing me. "Him?"

I swallowed. Her lips felt just as wonderful as I imagined a woman's would. As soft as butter. I felt her breasts against mine. I was melting against her.

She kept rubbing my clit, not letting up for a second. "You're so close. Just a few more rubs and licks and you'll be there. Please," she said. She sounded like she was begging.

Something in me was begging too. I walked to the window and looked out. She came up behind me. She was rubbing my breasts. I was letting her. I looked down below. People looked like bugs. They had no clue what was going on above their heads. My whole life was shifting.

She turned me around and exhaled on my nipples, and then she played with them using just her fingers. I watched them become hard. She took one in her mouth and sucked.

My legs felt weak. "I—I need to lie down," I said, pushing her away.

"Be my guest," she said, pointing to the bed. She began taking off her clothes, exposing full, perfect breasts, a narrow waist, and plump hips. She was a vision.

Then she became even more of one.

She sat on the bed, spread her legs wide, and touched her clit. She rubbed slowly. Then faster. Then slowly again. It was interesting to see her unique rhythm. She closed her eyes. Her face got red and scrunched up. She moaned—softly, not scarily like John had. She made beautiful sounds of pleasure. And no messy cleanup afterward either.

"Oh, fuck, that was good. So good to get rid of that stress. I just love making myself come." She smiled sneakily.

I was even hornier now and I knew that was her aim. As much as she'd wanted to come, she'd wanted even more to get me hot. Instinctively, I put a hand on my cunt. But she pushed it away.

"Allow me," she said.

She kissed up and down my legs and thighs—licking, kissing; breathing on my belly, her wet tongue against my increasing wetness, her soft tongue teasing, torturing my cunt with little flicks. She pushed a finger carefully into me. I gasped.

"See, you're not a freak," she said, staring at me with her soulful eyes. "Just a dyke."

I didn't have the presence of mind to think about the implications of those words so I focused instead on what she was doing.

She started licking my clit again. But she was going too slowly. It felt like being in the tub again. All buildup and no release. But then she went faster: up and down, clockwise, up and down and up and down and up and down. And then I felt it—a glorious release. Fireworks went off in my brain. There was simply no other way to describe it. I groaned. My legs vibrated. I screamed.

When it was all over, she touched a finger to my cunt.

"You are so wet," she said. "We must do something about that." Then she began lapping at me, which only made me more excited.

This was what sex was. This was why people wanted it constantly. I could see how you could become addicted. I could see how you could never want to leave your house again.

I could see why John liked those women on Cinemax.

John. He had no clue there was a live sex show he was missing. I smiled.

But it was more than just sex. I felt something for this woman. She was so funny, so caring. I could tell that, even though I hadn't known her long. And I could also tell that neither one of us would ever feel lonely again.

She curled up on the bed. I leaned up against her; my clit was right up against her beautiful, round ass. I wanted to enjoy this calmness forever, but I felt like I still needed more.

"I think I need to come—again," I said.

"Ahh. I've created a monster," she said, laughing. "Follow me," she said, and grabbed my hand.

Together, we walked to the tub. I positioned myself on the stream and felt her spooning me from behind. Now, she was pressing against me. She grabbed my breasts and kneaded them as the water caressed my clit. *Heaven.* That was the only word for this. Then, with no warning whatsoever, I felt a massive orgasm breaking free inside of me, filling my heart with passion. And as I recovered, Maxie kissed the back of my neck, filling my heart with love.

THE ST. GEORGE HOTEL, 1890

Lillian Ann Slugocki

It was an Edward Hopper landscape, and by that I mean infused with a dense yellow light, as if it was always fall, with dry leaves on the ground. There was a loneliness, and a distance between each human being, and always a sense of anonymity. I am an old woman now but I remember it as if it were yesterday. I was a rancher, a widow. It wasn't an easy life by any means, but I had my animals; Blue Bell, my tabby; and of course the big sky.

I went into town twice a month for supplies. By town I mean a strip of old buildings hard alongside the railroad tracks: the courthouse, a dry goods, a church, and the post office. I could always count on the sun and the wind to follow me wherever I went. At the end of the day, it was my custom to stop at the St. George Hotel, at the very end of the street. Even in those days it was dilapidated, but I admired Mildred, who tried, despite the sanguinity of the townspeople, to instill a little elegance into the shabby little town. She served high tea every Tuesday: elegant little sandwiches, dark tea, lemon tea, and tiny little pastries she baked herself.

In those days, I was about thirty-nine years of age, but not a bad specimen by any means: my breasts were still high and taut and my limbs tight, from hours and hours of labor out in the fields. And, to be delicate, I had begun to miss a man's company in my bed, and had taken to pleasuring myself beneath my heirloom quilt, usually late at night. I didn't fantasize about anything in particular; it was a ritual like spring cleaning, using vinegar to get the windows sparkling, baking soda to take out stains in the carpet, or petroleum jelly to polish the faucets. It had to be done, and so I developed the most efficient method possible, index finger squarely on my privates, and a slow circular motion, around and around, then faster and faster. When I finished, I would wash myself in the bathroom, turn out the lights, and go to sleep. We didn't speak about having a sex life in those days, it just wasn't done. You did what you could or you did without. End of story—or so I thought.

That fateful afternoon, I stopped in at the dry goods store, and ran into Tommy, who managed the cattle ranch down the road.

"Good day to you, sir," I called out.

"Madam," he said, tipping his hat.

At that moment, a tall man entered with a burn scar on his face, and I was drawn to it immediately—like a bolt of lightning, a zigzag of flesh from the upper right quadrant of his forehead, ending just below his left eye. It looked as if he had done battle with the gods, and won. Tommy leaned over to me and whispered, "That there is Kenyon-Something-Or-Other, half Indian, one hundred percent pissed off. I'd steer clear of him, for sure."

I tapped Tommy on the shoulder and said, "I expect since I've been taking care of myself for five years now, I'll be fine."

But when I walked out, I couldn't help but take another look at Kenyon and his scar. He was at the back end of the store, getting flour and sugar measured out. He was half Indian but he wore a battered cowboy hat and parti-colored beads and shells around his neck, and when he looked up at me and met my gaze, I quickly averted my eyes and walked away. Heavens, the nerve of that man! But even in that moment there was no denying he had stirred something in me, something long dormant. I am speaking, of course, of the passion between a man and a woman.

Still, I was determined to make my way to the St. George Hotel and enjoy high tea with Mildred. I loved the deep blue walls of her salon, the wainscoting, but above all, I loved the portraits of cowboys, Indians, and gypsy girls that she had painted in her spare time and hung over the old brick fireplace. The salon had real white linen tablecloths and a large bay window that looked west over the prairie and pale horizon. Many times it was just Mildred and I—just as well, I would think, we were both widows, both tough as nails, both happy with each other's company.

On that afternoon, just as we were settling in, the two of us, eager for chitchat and gossip, the man with the scar walked in.

"That's Kenyon" Mildred said softly, "mean as a rattle-snake."

"Heavens, who is he?" I asked, my blood already hot.

"You don't want to know," she admonished, then called out to him, "Kenyon, what can I do you for today?"

He replied, "I believe I'd like a cup of tea."

Ignoring Mildred's obvious shock, he walked right up to me and said, "Madam, I don't believe we've had the pleasure."

"Sally O'Brian," I said, introducing myself, mesmerized again by the scar. "What happened to your face?" I asked a moment later. Thankfully, Mildred had four traveling salesmen checking in, all wanting hot showers, clean towels, and whiskeys all around, so she was otherwise engaged and not an obstacle to our conversation.

"Dust storm," he replied, "set my face on fire, why? It bother you?"

"No," I answered honestly, "not at all."

We locked eyes for the second time that day; mine were cat's eyes, green, sometimes hazel, a dash of silver when the light was bright. His were black, but blue black, edged in violet. I wasn't afraid of him at all.

By the time Mildred had finished with the traveling salesmen, I was on my way up to his hotel room. Seems he came to town twice a month to barter furs and gold coins. I remember the steep stairs, a worn wool runner, cheap brass lamps on rickety tables on each floor, a skylight, a small room on the third floor; an enormous bed, high off the ground, where he laid me down. Night had fallen—finally, I could run my index finger up and down the place where the fire had scarred his skin.

"Next time I want you wearing a dress," he breathed in my ear as he unhooked my coveralls, peeled off my long johns and camisole. When I was naked, he stood me up and carefully and slowly unpinned my hair—it fell down around my shoulders, first the right section, then the left—all the while stopping to kiss me between my legs and I blush to say this two decades later, but I trembled at his touch, and opened up as wide as a river delta. And I do not exaggerate when I say that when he mounted me, it was like the mustangs on the open prairie—anybody who has ever seen this, no matter how prurient, will say it is a majestic sight. And that's what we were, wild horses on that narrow hotel bed. That poor bed took such a thrashing, it's a wonder it didn't crack open like a walnut.

The next morning the sun shone right onto his beloved forehead. I curled up next to him, praising the universe for sending me such a man. We lay in a knot of brightly colored blankets edged in satin, blue and red and navy, ivory colored homespun sheets, and goose down pillows. The room itself was nothing fancy, but it still possessed a certain charm, homemade rag rugs on the polished wood floor gleaming like honey. To my right, a small gateleg table, inlaid with marble, and dead center in the room, over our bed, one square window with gingham curtains.

"Good morning, beautiful lady," he said as he opened his black eyes, squinting some because the light was still shining down on him.

"I was just thanking the universe for sending me such a man, a real man," I whispered, caressing his cheek, and that gorgeous scar.

"I'd like to thank you by doing this..." and he slipped first one, then two fingers deep inside of me. I gasped, but then there was a knock on the door, and Mildred called out, "Room service, one pot of hot coffee."

I panicked and whispered, "Don't let her in. I don't want her to see me like this! She warned me about you!"

Mildred shook the door handle. "Kenyon! I had to get my derriere out of bed at seven A.M. to fix this coffee, and pour this coffee, and carry it up to your room, so you will open this door!"

He turned to me, practically pushing me out of the bed, and said, "Hide!"

Without thinking, I scrambled under the bed, naked as a jaybird, and he threw the covers down, so she couldn't see me. I heard him walk to the door and open it. "Mildred O'Connor, you are a pushy woman, can't a man have a piss?"

Then she said, "Listen you old rattlesnake, pay your bill and make yourself scarce, you hear?"

After she left, I crawled out from underneath the bed, wrapped myself in a sheet, and asked, "Why does she hate you so?"

"Ah," he said, dismissively, "some women went missing up beyond the ridge of the mountains, next town over, but it's nothing."

"What women?" I asked.

He responded by kissing me, and all sense and reason flew out of my brain, all notion of time. We started in again, worshipping our bodies. Night fell, and he was taking me slowly, from behind, in even, measured strokes. I thought my nipples were going to pop, as if I might burst out of my skin.

"Hurry," I said to him, "hurry please!"

"No," he replied, as pulled himself out.

"No," he said again, as he put himself in.

"No," he said, as he pulled himself out, "slow and sweet is the true road to paradise."

But I had to scream, I had to—the pleasure was so intense. I buried my face in the goose down pillow, hollered for dear life, and then it started—my first orgasm with a man, deep in the belly, like a rumbling, then it felt like lightning spreading down my legs. And with every stroke, my fists clenched and unclenched, and then he asked, "Aren't you on the road to paradise?"

"Glory hallelujah," I said, gripping him tighter. "Sweet Jesus, you know I am—" but I couldn't speak anymore, the orgasm had reached its pinnacle. I arched my back; it was almost painful, as if a demon possessed us, controlled us. I didn't think it was natural, and then I must've passed out because the next thing I remembered was moonlight, soothing, almost cool on my cheek as it poured into the open window from the dark sky over our heads.

When I looked down again, into the room, I saw her, a ghost—a beautiful woman with blood staining her tattered blue gown. She said, "You must leave his bed immediately."

"What are you talking about?" I asked.

"He kills all his women on the third night."

"But we're on the top floor!"

"Do what your must!" she warned.

And then her image faded, but I knew she spoke the truth. I suddenly realized I knew the real story about the lightning bolt, and quite frankly, I was scared to death. Stealthily, quietly, I tied together the ends of two blankets, and slipped out the window of the hotel, dangled for a moment, one story above the ground, regained my equilibrium, and carefully climbed down my knotted rope. I considered running back and warning Mildred, but I didn't. I only know this: I escaped with my life. I had my first and only orgasm in the St. George Hotel, forty years ago, with a monster. Funny: sitting here in another city, far, far away, I am still drawn to that scar.

THE LUNCH BREAK

Saskia Walker

What can I get you?"

I glanced up from my pocket mirror and when I saw the attractive waitress who watched and waited, I was so startled that I dropped my lipstick. Her gaze was direct, fearless, and powerfully sexual. My body responded instantly, my pulse rate rising.

"Coffee, please, and a club sandwich." I scrabbled for the lipstick. Her eyes never left mine, but she leaned down to the table and shifted the ashtray, nudging the lipstick back in my direction.

"Oh, I just bet you take your coffee sweet and strong," she whispered, low.

"Yes," I replied, mesmerized. "I do."

She gave me a dazzling smile, then turned and walked away, her hips cutting a rhythmic path through the low-slung tables and chairs in the sedate lounge bar. I sat back and watched, my fingers toying idly with the fitted jacket of my business suit, which lay abandoned over the arm of the chair. I had stopped in at Kilpatrick's, the salubrious and rather austere London hotel, after the meeting with my client, the hotel's publicity officer. He was sold on my advertising proposals and I was on a high. I just knew that if I had gotten behind the wheel of my Land Rover in that state, I'd have picked up another speeding ticket, so I stayed on to chill for a while. With the attention I was now getting from the waitress, it looked as if chilling wasn't going to be an option.

When she delivered my order, she threw me another look filled with pure, raw, sex appeal. She turned my cup in its saucer, facing the handle toward me. Her name badge announced that she was called Martine.

"I'm testing out some new cocktails for the bar. Why don't you drop by before you leave and I'll give you a taste of something good." She winked. *Well, that was direct.* I felt the tug of the woman's invitation from the pit of my stomach to the tip of my clit.

"Thanks, I'll do that, Martine."

I mustered a nonchalant smile, my fingers ruffling through my short, cherry-dyed crop, and watched as she walked away, her hips skirting obstacles. She knew that I watched. She stretched her legs back as she bent over the tables, the scalloped edge of her black skirt brushing tantalizingly high against the backs of her thighs, offering a glimpse of what appeared to be stocking tops. Her body was lush and curvy, her mouth a ruby pout. She cast sidelong glances back to me, her finger flicking quickly against the corners of her bow tie, before smoothing slowly over her fitted waistcoat.

I barely touched the sandwich; my appetite had been redirected toward the waitress. I had never been approached by a woman as forthright and blatant as her before—or as glamorous. It was one of those rare encounters when fizzing chemistry instantly anchors two people together. The situation made me very hot, but could I act on it? I was supposed to be in work mode. *What the hell.* Of course I could act on it!

Martine smiled and her eyes flashed a welcome from under heavy eyelashes when I climbed onto the bar stool in front of her. She was a total sex bomb, with thickly fringed, dark brown eyes and blue-black hair clipped up at the back of the head. The occasional glossy coil escaped to hang tantalizingly over her eyes, giving her subtle cover as she glanced around. There were signs of an alternative edge beneath her smart uniform. She had an electric blue streak in her hair, both her ears were fully studded, and there was evidence of a nose piercing. I liked that. I also had a streak of die-hard glam-punk that refused to conform, despite my career. Through the thin white sleeves of her shirt, I could make out her tattoos flexing as she went about her business behind the bar, rapidly shaking a cocktail mixer in such a physical way that her figure was shown off to perfection. I imagined what it would feel like to be pressed hard against her, to rub against her naked breasts and touch her in between those strong thighs. Maybe we would exchange contact info. Maybe we could meet, later on. My sex was heavy with the idea of it, the sensitive flesh crushed inside my G-string plump and swollen.

Martine set up a tall glass in front of me, gave the cocktail mixer a final dramatic shake, and poured me out a long, tall drink over crackling ice, popping in a smart black swizzle stick. She rested two provocatively speared cherries on the edge of the glass at the last moment, then pushed it over.

"A new recipe, please have some...and tell me what you think. Compliments of the bar." She gave me another wink. Her accent was heavy, either French or Italian.

I sipped the vibrant red-orange drink, looking at the waitress over the two plump cherries. Martine watched, her lips slightly open, a devilish look in her eyes. The cocktail hit the back of my throat; it was ice-cold and zappy, exhilarating, instantly making me wet. I could taste cranberry juice and other fruits—grenadine, vodka, and something else, a mystery ingredient I could not identify.

"Mmm…what is it?"

"It is Martine's version of Sex on the Beach," she replied, putting one hand on her hip and the other elbow on the bar, resting her chin on her hand as she looked directly into my eyes. "Shall we call it…Sex in My Bedroom?"

She is definitely coming on to me. I felt a rush of heat traversing my body, right from the tips of my toes to the roots of my hair. Was it the effect of the cocktail or the provocative woman who had made it for me?

"Do you think you'd like that…sex in my bedroom?" she added, her voice low. *Wow, direct wasn't the word!* My heart was racing. I breathed deep, trying to order my thoughts. I had never had such a direct come-on—this was one express lady. What would she be like in bed?

"I think I'd like to try it," I replied. Martine's mouth slid into another wide grin.

"I'm due for my lunch break."

I almost dropped the glass on the bar. *She meant now?* I glanced at my watch. I was due back at the office in just over an hour. I had promised to catch Jack, my boss, before he left for a board meeting. Martine toyed with a swizzle stick, eyeing my cleavage. My body thundered out its response.

"Okay," I managed. "Let's do it."

She turned to the barman working the other end of the bar and called out some instructions to him in French. He nodded and waved. She turned back to me, her eyes smoldering. God, she was hot. I wanted to find out exactly how hot.

"Come to room fourteen, lower ground floor, in three minutes." She pulled up a key chain from her hip, put a key into the register, and logged herself off. "I have only forty minutes for lunch break though," she added, lifting her eyebrows suggestively.

Perfect. I could be back at work in time.

The three minutes seemed to drag but gave me enough time to consider taking flight. I stayed put. Just a few minutes earlier, I had been reflecting on my business meeting. Now, well, now I was on Martine's lunch break with her. I glanced at my watch and swore low under my breath. It was time. I threw back the rest of the drink and stood up.

I clutched my jacket and portfolio against my chest and hurried down the stairs marked STAFF ONLY. I couldn't quite believe I was doing it, lurking in the hidden corridors of a premier London hotel, heading to an illicit meeting with a sex bomb with whom I had exchanged only a handful of words. A deviant thrill fired my veins.

Perhaps I would wake up.

And then there it was, room 14. From inside I could hear the distinct and powerful drum and bass sound of industrial dance music. I took a deep breath.

"Come on in," a voice shouted out when I rapped on the door. I turned the handle and pushed the door open. The room was filled with clutter, a metal-framed bed surrounded with stacks of clothes and teetering piles of books; lamps, bric-a-brac, and cushions covered the spaces between. Even the walls were covered with posters, photographs, mirrors, and other paraphernalia. A scarlet sarong was draped across the metal head of the bed, a vivid dash of color in the gloom. Over the bed, a poster of

Annie Lennox at her most androgynous grinned cheekily down from the wall. In the center of it all was Martine, sitting on the bed with her legs coiled under her. She chuckled, leapt up, and walked over. She rested one hand on my bare upper arm, stroking me, sending wild threads of electricity between us. I caught a breath of her perfume, something musky and wild.

"What do they call you, Red?" She nodded up to my hair.

"Kim," I replied, smiling.

"Kim, huh...well, Kim, I like a woman who goes after what she wants." Her tone was admiring.

Wait a minute. Me? *Did I really go after her?*

I had responded to her, I couldn't deny that, and I had found my way down the stairs, so I guess I was guilty. Martine growled low in her throat, eyeing my body. The atmosphere positively crackled between us.

"I admire your directness, too," I replied. "Thank you for your invitation, it made me very...hot."

Martine grinned proudly and pulled me into the room by one arm, closing in on my mouth for an urgent kiss as the door slammed shut. Her mouth was lush and hot, damp and inviting. My portfolio clattered to the floor. She backed me toward the bed, her eyes sparkling.

"You have to do it, when it happens like this, yes, or you will have a regret, and life it is too short for regrets, huh?"

She flickered her eyebrows at me. Before I had a chance to reply, she pushed me back and I landed on the bed on my back. She moved like lightning, her hands homing in on the heat of my sex, to the wetness that she knew awaited her. I opened my legs, my skirt riding up.

"Take your clothes off, quickly!" I stripped off my skirt and started to pull my top up and over my head while Martine pulled my silk G-string down my legs. The shelves behind us rattled and something fell; the stereo jumped onto the next track. My blood surged with a dangerous, dizzy rush of exhilaration when Martine stroked my legs and moved straight into my heat, taking my clit in her mouth, nursing its fullness and sucking deeply. She moved her mouth over my flesh in deliberate sweeps, ending back on my clitoris, with the tip of her tongue circling it closely, firmly. *Oh, she was good.* I felt as if a bomb was about to go off inside me.

That's when I noticed the mirror that stood close to the bed and the scene reflected there transfixed me. Martine was kneeling between my legs, and as her skirt rode up, I saw she wore stockings but no panties, her pussy naughtily peeping out as she bent. I could just make out the tip of her tongue, darting out and rolling over my sticky sex folds. It looked so strange, seeing myself like that, with her on me, and it sent me flying toward meltdown point.

"Oh, fuuuuuck…"

Martine lifted her head. Her fingers replaced her mouth and she plowed them inside me. Her free hand crept up to my bra, and she bent its cups down, setting my breasts free.

"You want it, don't you?" she asked, as her fingers tweaked at my nipples, bringing me nearer. She kicked off her shoes and slid her body down with her pussy pressed up against my bare thigh.

"Oh, fuck," I murmured again, when I felt the beautiful wet slide of Martine's heat on my leg. A wave of pleasure rushed up, the first ebbs of my orgasm.

"You're so hot," she said and her eyes were aflame. She began to move her hips, pressing her sex along my thigh, rubbing frantically. "I'm going to come too!"

We exchanged a look of total mutual appreciation, both moving desperately, climbing over the threshold. I let my hands close tightly on Martine's shoulders and pressed my leg up into the hot wet valley of flesh that rode me. Martine's lips parted and her eyes closed. She ground her hips down and pressed home. With a sudden cry, she came. My core pounded with release, my clit a buzz of sensation.

After a few moments of labored breathing, my head rolled to look back at the mirror. Did Martine put it there on purpose to entertain her lovers? I suddenly wanted mirrors everywhere; I wanted to see sex from every angle. Looking back, I saw that Martine had stood up and unzipped her skirt, quickly dropping it on the floor to one side. She threw off her bra as she went over to the wardrobe that stood in the gloomiest corner of the room, and rustled around inside. When she turned back, I didn't know where to look first: at the bright silver barbells that pierced through both her nipples or the enormous strap-on cock hanging from one hand.

She walked back and held it out. I took it in my hand, my eyes on stalks as I examined the huge contraption. It was molded with distended veins and the head was huge, engorged, as if it was about to explode. I ran my fingers around the edge of the head, imagining that rubbing against me, inside. My sex clenched.

"Wow," I murmured, looking up at Martine.

"You like it, huh?"

"It's um...amazing!"

"You must put it on."

"Me?" I blurted.

"Yes, I need more," she demanded, impatiently. The last round was obviously just for openers. I glanced at the clock; there was still time. Martine was already laid out on the bed, with her knees pulled up and her legs open. She had two fingers up to the hilt inside her sex, thrusting vigorously. Her breasts had rolled out to the sides. The piercings made her nipples look loaded, like twin torpedoes about to be launched. Between her legs, her fingers were slick with wetness.

I stood over her, filled with a sudden sense of longing and something else: power, raw power ebbing up from deep inside me. I hadn't worn a cock before. What would it be like? I felt a surge of vitality roar up inside me. I was going to fuck this woman, really fuck her. *Hard.* I stepped back and quickly climbed into the strap-on, pulling the holster tight against my pussy and between my buttocks. The thing felt heavy against my intimate parts, and outrageously large. I turned to glance at myself in the mirror, gasping when I saw it in profile. It looked totally strange and perverse in its size, brazen.

"I look obscene," I whispered to myself, a dart of sheer depravity flying around my veins.

Martine moaned from the bed, reaching out for me, her gaze on the cock. Christ, this was so hot! I knelt down between Martine's open legs and took a taste of her. She was so wet and tasted so good, her nectar creamy and warm. She shuddered against my face while my tongue explored her. I had one hand on the cock, the other over one of her breasts. I captured the knotted skin between thumb and forefinger, rolling the steel barbell between my fingers. I was gratified to hear her moans growing louder. I lifted my head to suck on the other nipple, my tongue toying with the barbell, and moved my hips between hers. Martine looked down when I whispered her name. I guided her hand over the huge head of the molded object, lubricating it with her wet fingers.

"Oh, yes, now," Martine urged. I began to edge the massive head of the cock into the slippery entrance to her sex, angling my hips to ease the upright cock inside.

"Oh, *mon dieu*," Martine cried out.

I groaned. "Can you take more of it?"

"Yes!" As if to confirm it, she grabbed the cock and hit a switch at its base. I gasped with shock when it started to vibrate, reverberating between us and sending a little jagged riff that went straight up into my clit.

Oh, my!

I was wired, hugely aroused, and totally empowered. I looked down at the woman spread in front of me, all wet with sex and wanting. She was like a pool of liquid lust on the bed, bubbling up, ready to be brought off. A sense of sheer and absolute power traversed my body. I pulled the base of the cock up against my clit with both hands, enjoying the weight and the vibrations there, where I was taut and pounding. The molded thing in my hands felt like a weapon and I jutted my hips forward, reaching and testing the tender succulent flesh of Martine's hole. I worked my hips slowly, edging it inside. Martine's hands flew up to the metal bed frame to brace herself. She began to rock in turn with my thrusts.

"Oh, yes, push hard," she mumbled. I lifted myself onto my arms, pushing the strap-on firmly against the resistance it met. She suddenly grabbed at my arms. Her hips bucked wildly. I leaned forward, watching the reflection of our bodies in the mirror, the line of my breasts heaving up as I moved back and forth between the other woman's thighs. It looked so hot. I was fucking her; I was fucking this hot glam-bitch with an enormous strap-on cock. My sex was on fire with arousal, the threat of another climax trembling right down into my hard-working thighs.

"Oh, Kim, I like you lots!" she cried out, gasps of pleasure and laughter escaping her. Her neck arched up, her eyelids lowering. She was so close.

"I like you lots too," I replied, grinning, loving her foreign tongue, and thrust hard. She reached down to the juncture of our bodies, rubbing her clit. The fingers of her free hand fastened over my nipple, pinching me while she bucked up. The pinch traversed my body, wiring itself into the heat between my thighs, and I had to fight the urge to shout my pleasure aloud. I looked down at the bucking woman beneath me and grabbed the base of the cock, crushing my clit hard against it, sending us both right over the edge.

Non, je ne regrette rien. I hummed the old Edith Piaf number as I hauled my Land Rover into its bay in the underground car park at HQ and stepped out, grabbing my portfolio.

"Hey, Kim, how did it go?" Jack was waving over to me as he threw his briefcase into his Merc. I had caught him just before he left for the board meeting. What a bonus.

"Success! They went for the whole campaign, web slots and all." It was a massive contract for the company, my best work to date.

"Excellent, I knew you'd pull it off. That pay raise of yours is secure."

He saluted as he climbed into the car and then stuck his head out of the window. "And you be sure you take yourself a good lunch break, you deserve it!"

I smiled to myself as I headed for the lift. *Too right, honey.* I had just enjoyed the best lunch break I'd ever had, and with a pay raise in the offing, I could afford to visit Kilpatrick's for lunch more often—just as Martine had suggested I should. Now how was that for staff motivation?

MEMPHIS

Gwen Masters

He was my best friend's husband. He was the consummate family man. This was just a friendly dinner, like all the others we'd shared. Hadn't he just called her and said he was having dinner with me?

So surely he didn't mean what he'd just said. Surely not.

"An affair..."

Or maybe I didn't hear him right.

I stopped halfway through the motion of spearing a lettuce leaf with a sterling fork. We were in a ridiculously posh restaurant just south of Memphis, both of us feeling out of place among the chandeliers and wine stewards. I looked up at him, dumbstruck.

"What?" I was whispering and not sure why, as frozen as the ice chips the shrimp rested on. My eyes met his brown ones over his tilted wineglass, and he smiled at me.

"We're hiding from what we already know." He said it with absolute certainty.

I dropped my shrimp fork with a clatter of silver on china. Neither of us noticed.

Is that how it starts? How affairs begin? With a gesture or a word that suddenly turns an old friend into a lover, crying out above you in a rented bed somewhere on the edge of nowhere? Does it always drop out of the blue and explode, fragmenting your life? And then plant itself inside you and grow into beauty, into memories and smiles, building you into something stronger than you were?

For me, with my married lover, there's a bounce in my step that everyone notices but can't explain. It comes from pulling up beside a sports car parked outside of a hotel, in a town you've never visited before, and going through an open door with the Do Not Disturb sign already in place. It comes from there being no time for words before you're rushed into a dimly lit room and surrounded by his arms, his voice, and his desire. You both collapse onto the bed that has become a refuge.

He's married. I knew that as I walked out of the restaurant and slid into the passenger seat of his sports car. I heard her name in my head as he drove, one hand on the wheel and one hand on my thigh. I saw her in my head as the hotel room door closed behind us. I listened to her laughing with him as he pressed me back against that door and kissed me. I felt the guilt as I kissed him back, but I wanted him more than I wanted to heed the conscience that was shaking its head in shame.

I didn't hate her. I didn't even want to hate her. She's my best friend. She's a good wife, a good mother. She's a better woman than I am. She didn't deserve this.

I slipped off his wedding band and it dropped to the floor.

His hands cradled my face. His tongue danced with mine. He groaned low in his throat, the music of it resounding in my head, telling me this wasn't wrong. My hands found the lapels of his black suit jacket and I slid the silky material over his broad shoulders, letting it drape down his arms and catch his hands a moment before falling into the pool of darkness behind him. The top button of his dress shirt opened as easily as if I'd undressed him a thousand times.

I need this, I thought, as I began to undress him. He stood looking down at me, towering over me. I suddenly remembered that his wife was taller than me. I wondered about how they'd look together in bed. The thought filled me with an inexplicable anger. I wondered if he felt guilty, but I found I didn't really care.

I looked up at him as my hands continued to work. "Anything she does, I'll do. Anything she doesn't do for you, I will do it, over and over."

He smiled a slow smile. "I know."

My dress fell to the floor. I stood before him unashamed, the younger woman, the adulteress. The kind of woman that other women call a whore, whispering behind their hands. I found I really didn't care what anyone else might think of me.

Before his slacks hit the floor, my hand was wrapped around his cock. I pushed all thoughts of her from my mind as I opened my mouth over him. He groaned and buried his shaking hands in my hair, thrusting gently between my lips as I sucked him with the flat of my tongue, wanting to do everything he could imagine a woman ever doing to his body.

I slid my mouth up to his swollen head and slowly sank back down. He pulled my hair back from my temple so he could watch as he disappeared into my mouth. I flicked my tongue quickly across the sensitive skin just below the head of his cock and he bucked into me on pure instinct. My hands slid up his thighs and found his balls, heavy and surprisingly tight with anticipation. His head fell back as I sucked him harder, faster, letting my fingers play over him.

He said my name.

I began to pump him in and out of my mouth at a steady rhythm, my only goal being to taste the nectar that I knew would be as unique as he was.

He groaned as he came, a desperate sound muffled by his shoulder. His hands tightened in my hair as I took his essence into my mouth, let it flood my tongue. I sucked harder, feeling the spasms against my tongue. I moaned aloud at the pleasure of his juices sliding thickly down my throat. He watched with fire in his dark eyes.

He was still hard. He pushed me back on the bed and gently spread my legs. I closed my eyes as his fingertip touched me—and the last traces of guilt fled as he licked slowly upward, teasing my clit with the tip of his wet tongue. I opened underneath him, the wanton slut, willing to do anything to please a man. His hands tenderly worshipped my body, cupping my breasts and molding them, flicking my hard nipples with his calloused thumbs. His lips nibbled at my thighs and his tongue curled around my clit to suck me like I'd just sucked him. He pressed one long finger into me and moaned.

"I want to fuck you. I've wanted to fuck you for years."

I bucked into his hand and he obliged by sliding two fingers into me. Without question as to whether I would like it or not, he pressed one finger against the tiny hole below my slit, pushing the length of his finger deep into my ass. I arched up into him, more than willing to do anything he wanted, whether he asked or not. He rubbed his fingers together through the thin wall of my body and sucked hard on my clit.

I came hard. I tried to catch my breath but all I could do was hold it while I let the tremors build. My pussy clenched tight on his hand and he moved his fingers within me, searching out every last drop of desire that flowed from me and onto his tongue. His name was a moan on my lips as my fingers tangled in his dark hair—to pull him closer or to push him away, I didn't know. He held my legs open when I closed them, trying to control the feelings coursing through me. He licked me harder. What I thought would be pain turned into pleasure and I came again, this time harder than the last. Through the red haze that had consumed my mind, I vaguely knew that he was pulling away from me so that he could watch as my body convulsed without shame or modesty.

Then his hands were touching me everywhere, cradling me like a delicate sculpture. His breath came harsh and ragged against the curve of my belly. He rose above me, pushing my legs apart to accommodate what he needed. He sat on the bed between my thighs and looked down, hands caressing my calves.

"You still want this?"

"I can't live without it," I answered, with more honesty than I'd ever felt.

I watched as he picked up a shiny gold packet. I took it from his hands and opened it, the tearing sound confident and soothing. Together we slipped the protection over him. He moaned as I stroked him.

"I want you inside me." I almost begged.

He pressed his hard erection against me. I spread my legs and we both looked down, watching as he pressed his hips forward. I felt his head slide into me and I watched as the rest of him followed, feeling him fill me, stretching my body around him.

"Don't make me wait anymore," I pled.

He pulled back...thrust forward...and my hips began to move with his. We found the rhythm we needed together. Every motion of my body brought him deeper into me, so deep that I cried out with the surprise and pleasure of it. His hands moved over me, touching my neck, cradling my shoulders, caressing my legs as I wrapped them around him. We began slowly, building into something faster, until he caught my hands in his and pressed them to the bed above my head.

He drove into me, hard and vicious. I cried out, not caring who heard me. The muscles of his back tensed and relaxed under my calves as he pumped me. He buried his head in my shoulder and took me with no gentleness, but with a rough possessive-ness—near anger almost—that left me shaking with pleasure. I met every thrust until he became too rough for me to match his power, then I wrapped myself tightly around him and closed my eyes, another orgasm building. He released my hands as he felt my contractions.

My body felt like liquid fire. I exploded around him, exploded with a cascade of color behind my eyelids. I whimpered his name into the quiet of the room. I wrapped my hands in his hair, holding him close to me. I bucked mindlessly against him, completely under his control.

He followed my climax, letting the pulses of my orgasm drive him over his own edge. I felt him throb deep within me as he came, heard his deep raspy voice call my name. His fingers clenched the sheets and his teeth seized my neck, biting down as the last of his orgasm washed over him.

He went limp and supple against me and slowly lowered himself to cover me. His weight pressed our bodies together. Our breath burned as it filled our lungs.

I slid my hands through his hair again and again, soothing him, feeling his breathing ease and his heartbeat slow. He shifted his hips and pulled out gently, leaving me aching with the void.

I let my legs drop and stretched them out beside his longer ones, feeling the tingle in my muscles.

He pulled a blanket over us and snuggled in behind me, his face buried in my neck. The tip of his nose was cold in contrast to the heavy heat of the rest of him.

After a few moments of lightly caressing the hands that were linked around my waist, I asked, "How long do we have?"

It was a moment before he spoke. "She won't be back from New York until Tuesday."

"Two days," I whispered.

"Will you stay here with me?"

I turned to face him in the bed. I traced the tiny lines of his forehead with my fingertip. I thought about what my answer would mean, about whether or not it was wise to continue. I waited for the guilt to come, braced myself for it, and only found certainty and a slight sadness.

"I'll stay," I said simply.

Thus began a new phase of my life, that of lover and mistress to a married man. I should feel shame, a desperate need to redeem my self-respect. At least, that's what the women who whisper behind their hands think I should feel.

I feel sorry for those who don't have what I've discovered, for those who can't feel the passion and rebirth I've found. I have moments of guilt. I can't avoid that little voice in my head, that annoying insistence on being morally straight.

I take full responsibility for what I'm doing.

Tomorrow I'll see his wife. She and I will have lunch. I'll listen as she shares tidbits of her life: the escapades of her young children, the latest headaches of her job. She'll be as lovely as ever with her beautiful red hair and her skin like fine china. She'll complain about having a man who works so much. She will look at me, her friend, and share secrets.

And I'll share with her, everything and anything I feel like sharing...with the exception of one thing.

I'll smile as I don't tell her that last night I fucked her husband in a hotel bed in Memphis.

I'll laugh at her jokes as I don't tell her that I will be on a plane as soon as I pay our tab, heading to a hotel room in Birmingham where he is giving a presentation. When he's done I'll undress him.

I'll make love to him right after he calls to tell her goodnight.

As she puts the children to bed, I'll be riding him in a hotel room, making him cry out my name and forget all about her.

My conscience is clear. I'll lose no sleep as I lie beside him.

I told you: she's a better woman than I am.

Remember?

THE OTHER WOMAN

Kristina Wright

It was Jason's fantasy, not mine; Jason's desire for a three-some—two women and him, of course—that had me sitting in a hotel bar nervously sipping on my second cosmopolitan in less than an hour. We were waiting for the woman who would be our third and I was wishing I was anyplace else but there.

Jason grinned like a teenaged boy seeing his first dirty movie. He reached across the bar and squeezed my hand. "Thanks for doing this, doll," he said. "Who knows, maybe you'll get what *you* want for your birthday."

Ultimately, it had been the allusion to an engagement ring that had me sitting there in the first place. My hands were clenched in my lap so I wouldn't fidget. When I'd agreed to Jason's ménage à trois birthday request, he'd immediately known whom to ask. I wondered if all men were like that—they had a name and number always at the ready, in case the opportunity should present itself.

I glanced toward the entrance for about the fiftieth time since we had walked into the hotel bar. It had been Jason's idea to meet me here a few minutes before the other woman arrived and my idea to get a hotel suite for the night. I just couldn't bear the thought of him sleeping with the other woman in our bed. Somehow, having a threesome in a five-star hotel felt more like a fantasy than any part of my reality—and that was exactly how I wanted to think of it. Just a fantasy, nothing real that could hurt my relationship with Jason. The other woman would come and go and we would still be intact, untouched. Or so I hoped.

I kept thinking of her as the other woman, even though I knew her name was Stephanie and she worked in the accounting department at Jason's firm. I would be face-to-face with Stephanie-from-accounting and I wasn't sure what the etiquette was for that. What do you say to a woman you've never met but intend to fuck before the night is out?

I must have looked as nauseous as I felt because Jason asked, "You're not going to back out on me, are you?"

I wanted to tell him to go screw himself, but a woman was coming toward us and, somehow, I knew it was Stephanie. She had the long brown hair and cute smile Jason had described, but she wasn't what I expected. Not gorgeous, like I'd imagined; not untouchable, as I'd been afraid. She looked friendly, kind, like someone I might have known once a long time ago—familiar in a way I couldn't quite place.

"Hi," she said, and even her voice had a Southern softness to it that seemed almost touchable. "I'm sorry I'm late."

Jason practically fell over himself trying to hold a chair out for her. "That's all right, we just got here."

I glared at him as she turned to hang her purse on the back of the chair. He just kept grinning that ridiculous grin.

Stephanie looked at me from under long lashes. "Hi," she said again. "It's nice to meet you, finally."

I arched an eyebrow at her. I wasn't feeling too charitable now, promise of an engagement ring or no. "Finally?"

I couldn't really tell in the dim light, but it looked like she blushed. "Jason is always saying how great you are. It's so nice to meet you at last."

I was torn between feeling jealous that this woman had been talking to my future fiancé without me knowing it and feeling good that he'd been saying nice things about me. "Thank you."

Jason ordered a bottle of my favorite Riesling and my annoyance melted away. I hadn't eaten much at lunch, so the wine went to my head pretty fast. By the time Jason suggested we go up to our suite, I knew Stephanie was five years younger than me, originally from Georgia, and just coming out of a bad marriage. She was about as sweet as honey and I couldn't make up my mind whether it was genuine or an act. It's hard to tell with Southern belles, sometimes. It didn't seem to matter when Jason put his arm around me and led me to the elevators. I felt good and I was determined to hang on to my mood.

Stephanie followed us into the elevator, standing close to Jason on the other side. His hand was on my hip making slow, teasing circles through the silky fabric of my skirt. I giggled nervously.

Jason leaned down and whispered, "What's funny?"

I rested my head against his shoulder. "I can't believe I'm doing this."

His hand stilled on my hip. "Don't think about it, Claire. Be a bad girl for once. You'll love it."

I honestly didn't think Jason had ever considered what I might love. I knew he was self-centered and I accepted that about him because he had so many other good qualities. I knew I wasn't the most beautiful or exciting woman he'd ever dated, and maybe I let him bully me a little too much to make up for that fact. At the moment, with two cocktails and several glasses of wine in my system and a strange woman following us into our suite, I was tired of being the good girl. He was right, I'd probably love being bad if I gave it half a chance.

"You don't have to convince me," I purred, reaching over to stroke him through his slacks as he opened the door. "You want a bad girl, you've got her."

I walked into the small sitting room of the suite and turned to see him holding the door for Stephanie. He put his hand on the small of her back as he led her into the room. The gesture was comfortable, familiar. Too familiar. In that moment, as they crossed the threshold into the luxurious suite that had been rented with only one purpose in mind, I knew Jason had already slept with Stephanie.

Funny thing, I didn't feel all that jealous. In fact, I wasn't even surprised. I'd often suspected him of sleeping around, but he accused me of being insecure. Now that I knew, I didn't feel anything at all. Maybe inviting Stephanie to join us in bed was his way of assuaging his guilt. If I okayed a threesome, maybe I'd okay their twosome.

I didn't have time to delve into the logic of Jason's behavior because I was standing in the doorway to the bedroom, holding on to the door frame. Jason didn't take much notice of me as he and Stephanie walked past me. She sat on the edge of the bed and he knelt beside her, reaching around to brush her long hair out of the way before softly kneading her shoulders.

She smiled softly at me and held out her hand. "Don't be shy," she said.

I should have told her to get her ass out of our room and stay the hell away from my man. That's what women do, isn't it? But I didn't. Instead, I crossed the room and took her hand. I never looked at Jason, but I could hear his breathing pick up, as if he could barely contain himself now that the fulfillment of a lifelong fantasy was close at hand.

Stephanie's hand was soft and warm. She rubbed my fingers lightly before trailing her fingertips up my arm. "Why don't you sit down?" she said, patting the bed. "You look a little wobbly."

I *was* a little wobbly, but I didn't know if it was from the alcohol or because of the way she was touching me. I'd never slept with a woman before, never had a threesome. I'd never wanted to. But something about Stephanie's soft touch felt as warm and familiar as her honey-sweet voice and I found myself wanting something I'd never contemplated before.

Even as I was thinking about kissing her, Stephanie leaned over and brushed her lips against my cheek. "He thinks this is for him," she whispered near my ear, her breath feathery light on my cheek. "But it's not. It's for us."

It seemed a silly thing to say while my boyfriend-almost-fiancé was reaching around to squeeze Stephanie's breasts as he nibbled on her neck. If it was for us, I sure as hell wasn't getting anything out of the deal.

Stephanie gently pushed Jason away from us both. "Hey, big guy, why don't you back up and give us some space?" Jason looked about to protest until she added, "Watch us for a little bit and then we'll let you join the party."

Jason's voyeuristic little heart must have been thumping happily at that. He scooted off the bed and went to the chair by the window. His erection was making a tent in his pants and he looked ridiculous. Stephanie rolled her eyes and I giggled. Jason looked at me sharply, as if warning me not to screw up his fantasy. I just shrugged and flopped back on the king-sized bed. I glanced at the darkness of the bare window, wondering who might be looking into the room from the next building over and what they might make of this scene. My usual modesty was gone and I had no desire to draw the blinds. I was going to bed with my boyfriend and another woman—modesty hardly seemed appropriate.

Stephanie curved her body around mine, her soft, full breasts pressing against my side. She reached under my blouse and lightly stroked my bare skin. I shivered and turned my head toward her. Suddenly, her mouth was there and we were kissing. Her lips were as soft and warm as her hands and she tasted of wine and strawberries. I hadn't thought kissing a woman could be so different from kissing a man, but it was. She was there, in the moment, not rushing ahead, not kissing me too hard. She nibbled my lips and sucked lightly on my tongue, all the while her hands stroked my body. She never touched my breasts or between my legs; she stayed in safe, neutral territory like a boy afraid to go too far for fear of being rejected.

It surprised me when I guided her hand to my breast. It seemed as if I needed her there, now, and if she wasn't going to do it, I was going to have to show her how. The feeling of her fingertips plucking gently at my nipple was marred only by Jason's low moan from the corner. I could hear a steady swish-swish sound and suspected he was masturbating. The mental image was sad and somehow pathetic, so far removed from the wonderful feelings Stephanie was giving me, I couldn't dwell on it. Instead, I hooked a leg around her hip and pulled her closer, drawing her body into mine until we were pressed together from tits to hips.

"Fuck her," Jason rasped. "Fuck her."

Stephanie ignored him, so I did, too. I was suddenly anxious to feel her naked body against mine. I pulled back far enough to unbutton her blouse and slip it over her shoulders. She fumbled with my blouse as well, each of us mirroring the other's movements until we were topless. Her nipples were dusky rose and large, half as large as her breasts. They were succulent and unique and I bent my head to taste them. I decided she must wear some kind of flavored body lotion because her breasts tasted like strawberries, too.

She fondled my breasts, kneading them roughly, and yet it didn't seem nearly as animalistic as when Jason did it. I whimpered softly and writhed against her as she pulled and twisted my nipples. I tugged her skirt up over her hips and felt the thong that ran up the crack of her ass. I slipped my fingers under it and tugged it up higher, knowing it was wedged into her pussy in a way that would be both pleasant and maddening. Funny how I knew so much about her simply because she was a woman. It was like knowing the secret handshake without being told.

My eyes closed when her mouth found my nipple. I whimpered again, clutching her long, silky hair in my hands. I opened my eyes to find Jason standing beside the bed, cock in hand, watching us. He looked...crazed. Wild. If I hadn't been so caught up in what Stephanie was doing to me, I might have been afraid of his alien expression.

Stephanie slid farther down my body, kissing and licking her way along my rib cage, across my belly. She braced her hands on my thighs and spread them wide. I could feel her breath between my legs and I tensed, waiting. For what, I wasn't sure. She could do anything she wanted to me, as far as I was concerned. As long as she didn't stop touching me.

Jason moved around to the end of the bed, so that he was behind Stephanie. I couldn't see his hands, but I could tell by the way she shifted that he was getting ready to fuck her. The thought of his sliding into her didn't anger me or arouse me, it just seemed like a bit of a nuisance, considering I wanted her attention for myself.

Stephanie looked up at me from between my thighs. I was still dressed, my skirt bunched high on my thighs. "I want to go down on you," she murmured, kissing my thigh. "Can I?"

She jolted forward and I knew Jason was in her. He looked at me over the top of her head. "Claire doesn't have orgasms," he said, and I could see the contempt—or was it pity?—in his eyes. "She can't."

The only thing I saw on Stephanie's face was lust. "She's never been with me," she murmured, too softly for him to hear.

She braced her hands on my thighs, spreading me wider and also anchoring herself against Jason's brutal thrusts. He was pushing her into me, driving us both farther up the massive bed. Stephanie hardly seemed to notice. She reached down and pushed my skirt higher. I felt her fingers rub me through my panties, petting me softly.

"Put your head back," she said. "Relax."

I did as she said, resting my head on the pillow and closing my eyes. Jason was fucking her furiously now, making the bed shake. I knew he wouldn't last long at that pace, even with a condom.

I felt cool air on my pussy and realized she'd pushed my panties to the side. I stiffened and tried to pull my thighs together, but she held me open. I felt her hair on my thigh a moment before her mouth lowered to my cunt. I was startled by the soft, wet sensation and I gasped.

Jason stopped moving. "I told you, that won't do anything for her," he said impatiently.

I felt Stephanie draw back and I bit the inside of my mouth to keep from begging her to stay. I hadn't wanted this anyway, this had been Jason's idea. I'd be damned if I'd beg this woman to lick me. It would only give Jason fuel for the next sexual fantasy he wanted to fulfill. As long as I didn't enjoy it, I was pretty certain I could make sure it never happened again.

But instead of leaving me, Stephanie only slid my panties down my legs. "You're getting what you want, Jason. Let me have what I want."

Jason didn't answer, but the bed started moving again. Stephanie's mouth found my clit and she sucked steadily, pausing only to dip her tongue into my cunt. I was wet, I knew that much. I also knew that her jaw would get tired long before I had an orgasm. I was aroused, really aroused, but I felt like I was going to cry from the feeling of need and frustration I knew all too well.

I heard a familiar groan and knew Jason was coming. I kept my eyes closed; I didn't want to see his face. I felt his weight shift off the bed and Stephanie seemed to melt into me, as if she'd been waiting for him to leave so she could really get down to business.

Her tongue, teeth, and lips devoured my cunt. I felt like a ripe fruit being sucked—I even sounded like it. I resisted the urge to close my thighs around her head, knowing she would only push me open again. I could feel something, a sensation of pressure, building low in my belly. I'd felt it before and recognized it for what it was, but it had always eluded me. Soon she'd get tired or I'd give up. I couldn't even make myself come, how could I expect anyone else to? That's what Jason was always saying.

Just on time, Stephanie moved her mouth away and rested her head on my thigh. I was still fighting the urge to cry, but I could feel the tears sliding down my cheeks anyway. I kept my eyes closed, wishing she would leave and Jason would get in bed with me. Then we could wake up in the morning and order room service and pretend this had never happened. But somehow, I didn't think he would feel the same way.

Stephanie trailed her hand over my thigh and across my mound. I quivered as her fingers spread my lips and she slid one into me. Her finger went in deep and hard, not as thick as a cock, but somehow more substantial. I jumped when she added a second finger. Soon, she was finger-fucking me with a hard, steady rhythm. Again, I tried to close my thighs and she held me open, working my cunt into a lather.

"That's so sexy," Jason muttered.

He was back in the chair, watching us. I tensed, but Stephanie soothed me with her other hand and gentle kisses on my thighs. When I relaxed, she fucked me harder.

It didn't take long before I was feeling something again. This time, it was more intense, closer to the surface. For the first time since I'd joined her on the bed, I was wondering if maybe Stephanie knew something I didn't. I tried to follow that feeling, but before I could reach it, she withdrew her fingers.

I grunted in frustration.

"Relax," she whispered, tonguing my belly. "You'll get there."

I didn't believe her, but I wanted to. God, how I wanted to. When her tongue returned to my cunt, I lifted my ass and thrust against her mouth. I wanted what she was teasing me with and I was starting to think I might actually get it. Suddenly, this no longer felt like some dirty little fantasy in an anonymous hotel suite—this was real and hot and I wanted it more than I had ever wanted anything in my life.

Stephanie sucked and licked and nibbled my pussy like she'd been doing it all her life. Maybe she had. I knew nothing about her except she was fucking my boyfriend. That should have made me angry. I should have been screaming and throwing things. Instead, I was digging my fingers into the sheets and writhing against her mouth.

"Why don't you come use that mouth on me?" Jason asked, his voice raspy with renewed lust.

Stephanie pulled away once again and I could have sworn she made a slurping sound. "Why don't you go in the other room and mix us some drinks? We'll be done in a few minutes."

I expected Jason to argue. Instead, he stood up and left the room.

Stephanie shook her head. "What an asshole."

"And you're sleeping with him."

She didn't look surprised that I knew. "I'm an idiot."

We both giggled. Then, ever so gently, she kissed my pussy. "Now, let me show you what it's all about."

"He was right. I can't. I mean, I don't." Ridiculous as the situation was, with me half-naked and spread out before her, I still blushed at my confession. "I don't want to waste your time."

Her throaty laugh was sexy as hell. "Honey, it's not a waste of time, it's an investment. Now, relax and come for me."

I wanted to say, if only it were that easy, but then she licked me again. Somehow, I didn't feel like arguing. I closed my eyes once more and let her eat me. She nibbled my clit until I thought I'd scream from pain, but the pain turned into something else, something more intense. She slid her fingers into me again, but this time she kept her mouth on my clit, working me inside and out until I couldn't separate the sensations. Over and over, she licked and fucked my cunt until I felt swollen and drenched. And as the sensations began to build, I knew I could come. And somehow, knowing it was enough to make it happen.

She sucked my clit into her mouth and worked her fingers deeper into my cunt, building up the momentum until my body tensed and the most amazing sensation I'd ever felt rippled through me, centering in my cunt.

I threw back my head and gasped and the gasp became a moan. Everything ceased to exist except my cunt and the mouth and fingers pleasuring it. And through it all, I kept thinking, *I'm coming, I'm coming, I'm coming.*

Stephanie nursed my clit gently as I came down from my orgasm. She was giggling and slurping and I was gasping and writhing against her mouth.

"Thank you, thank you," I whispered. "Oh, my god, thank you."

"Oh, hon, don't thank me. You are delicious." She slid up beside me until her body spooned mine on the big, soft bed. "You really are."

I wanted to ask her how she knew what to do, how she'd made me come when no one else ever had, including myself. But I was suddenly more tired than I'd ever been. One minute my body was throbbing and flushed and the next I was blinking groggily at the unfamiliar surroundings as a fully dressed Stephanie stroked my hair gently.

"Shh, go back to sleep," she said softly. "I'm going to go."

"Where's Jason?" I asked, feeling suddenly guilty for having forgotten all about him and even more guilty that I didn't really care.

"Jason fell asleep on the couch while we were busy." She shook her head. "He's a jerk, Claire. I'm sorry for getting involved with him."

I curled on my side, watching her like a contented cat. "Don't be. I suspected it. And besides, if you hadn't, I wouldn't have met you. And that would have been a tragedy."

We grinned at each other.

"Can I call you?" she asked.

I hadn't known how I'd handle it if Jason had wanted to do this again, but I really didn't know what to say to her. "I don't know. I don't think I could do this again. I'm not really a threesome kind of girl."

She sat on the edge of the bed and stroked my hair. "I didn't mean that, Claire. I meant, can I call *you*."

I looked up at her, thinking how she'd made me feel so good and never asked anything for herself. Then I thought of Jason, asleep in the next room. Would he care? Did he need to know? All the questions seemed meaningless.

"Yeah, call me," I said, pulling her face down for a kiss. "Soon."

TALKING DIRTY

Shanna Germain

We've come to this hotel twelve times, once a week for the last three months. There are other hotels in our area, but this is the one Cate likes best. It's the cleanest, she says. Everything is properly wrapped. Nearly pristine.

Cate stands next to me at the check-in line. Her hands wrap her elbows. She has to touch something of her own when she's nervous. Most of the time, her body is one of the safe things, one of the clean things. I want to put her in a protective bubble. Not like the Bubble Boy, but something sexy and sleek. A clear barrier that wraps her body and clings to her every curve. Something that would let her breathe. Not that she has physical trouble breathing. It's not asthma or anything like that. It's a mental clog in the airways that comes and goes, depending on Cate's weather.

"Ready?" I ask, when I have the key. It's the flat plastic keys they use now—a new one to each customer—and Cate doesn't mind them as much as the heavy metal ones.

"Ready, Freddy," Cate says.

"Honey," I say as we make our way to the elevator. "It has been too long. My name's Bobby."

She drops her voice just a little but doesn't acknowledge my joke. "Baby, I am so fucking ready. I can't even tell you." She doesn't have to. It's in those ice blue eyes, so pale that I sometimes think I can see through them. It would be enough to know that she wants this too. "What if this—?" she squeezes her elbows in with her palms, her arms making a square across her body.

"It's going to be fine," I say. And then, the thing she really needs to hear: "And even if it's not, *we'll* be fine. I promise." It isn't until I say it that I realize I need to hear it too.

The trip to the room goes smoothly. No one shares the elevator. I remember to use my key to push the elevator button. Even the hallway is clear—no porters or guests to throw Cate off.

When we get to the hotel room, we slip off our shoes and leave them in the hallway like dirty room service plates. There's the chance someone might steal them, but it's a small price to pay. I've brought extras in the car.

"Wait one sec," I say. Cate stands, hopping from bare foot to bare foot on the carpet, while I duck into the room and give it a once-over. It has to be a different room each time, or the trick doesn't work. This one is bigger than normal, but not so big that there's room for a couch. Which is good. The less fabric, the better. The bed is made as though no one's ever slept in it. Everything is arranged in perfect order—TV remote lined up straight with the edge of the nightstand, blank pad with the pen snugged up to it. Even the tiny cans of peanuts and Coke, never opened, looking like they've never been touched.

In the bathroom, I straighten the edges of the bath mat and make sure the toilet paper is still covered in its protective sleeve. It's a nice bathroom—L-shaped, with the shower framed in glass, clear and perfect. I put both bars of minisoap, safe inside their paper wrapping, on the sill of the tub. I turn the shower on full blast, making sure that the water is just warmer than body temperature. The spray turns the skin of my wrist bright pink.

I dry my hands on the very back of the towel, where she won't be able to see, and make sure the terry cloth hangs perfectly straight. Then I slip back out to where she stands in the hall, shifting from foot to foot, elbows in her palms.

"It's perfect," I say. Even if it wasn't, I would say this. She's willing to believe for me, to try, as long as I believe. If I show doubts, if I ask if it's okay, if she's okay, it starts the mechanism in her head. I think of it as a bomb—once it starts, you can't stop it until it explodes—but Cate says it's more like a clock, winding its unstoppable way up until she can't hear anything but the trill of the alarm.

I wish it was a clock, that easy. I'd hire someone to go in there and rework the wires, give that cuckoo bird a little shut-up surgery. But, of course, it doesn't work like that. The brain, as Cate's therapist says, is not a simple machine.

Cate smiles, but it's her nervous smile, the one where she pinches her bottom lip between her teeth. "Okay then," she says. "Let's do this. Boom-boom-boom."

I want to kiss her for trying to make a joke, but it's too early. I haven't even washed yet. "Come in to my room," I say as I pick her up and push the door open with my elbow. She closes her eyes as I carry her through into the bathroom.

"It's *up*," she says. "Come *up* to my room." Eyelids squeezed shut, her hands still holding her elbows. This is a tic in the ritual. I hold her there in the bathroom, her balled-up weight against my chest, waiting to see if this will throw us off course. My breath stays tight in my chest; it's been three weeks since we've made love. Last week, one of the minisoaps wasn't wrapped.

Before that, it was something she couldn't explain, the feeling that something was off. Once, we never even made it to the room—a man touched Cate's elbow in the elevator on the way up—and I just pushed the L button and we rode back down to the lobby without a word.

Cate inhales—a big sound that pushes her belly out. She pops her cheeks out like a chipmunk and wiggles her lips over her teeth. Holding her breath and counting down from ten. This is something her therapist's taught her, I think. A way to stop the wind-up. Sometimes it works. Sometimes it just makes her dizzy.

She opens those pale eyes.

"Okay, I'm good," she says. "Let's do this." Oh, god. Have I heard more beautiful words? No.

"You're fucking beautiful," I say.

"Okay, okay," she says. "Just get my beautiful ass in the fucking shower."

I want to laugh, to kiss her again. The therapist says she'd never heard of swearing as a way to cope, but that we are free to use it if it works. Sometimes it works. Cate only shakes a little as I lift her, still clothed, into the shower.

When she's standing, I close the glass door and stand outside the shower. Her body made wavy by the glass, Cate strips from head to toe, as she always does, and hands me the soaking clothes piece by piece. Hair tie first. Earrings. T-shirt, then lace bra. She leaves her wedding ring on. The pants come off, right leg first, then left. I put each of them into the garbage can without wringing them out. Last is the blue lace thong, the one I must have bought hundreds of over the years—I don't know what we'll do if they stop making that style and color. She hands it to me and then shuts the glass door. I turn away, busying myself with the wet fabric, the overflowing garbage can. I'm not allowed to see her until she's clean.

I undress quickly, standing around the corner from the shower so that she can't see me. In the hotel mirror, my face, my body. Wrinkles at the corners of my eyes and mouth. Good arms, strong shoulders. I'm still in shape, or I try to be. Hair graying at the chest. I didn't used to be so hairy. When we met—god, how long ago when we met—I was nearly hairless, such a skinny, smooth boy. That was before Cate's...before she changed...and I guess I can only be grateful that her compulsions don't extend to hair. I'd shave if she needed me to, of course I fucking would, but I'm suddenly, incredibly, in love with her all over again for allowing the brown and gray curls that cover my chest.

I sit on the toilet seat, cool against my ass, and listen to her wash. My cock is growing hard just from the *sucka-sucka* of the suds against her body, from knowing that she's washing every part of her, top-down. Right now, it's the long circles of soap and water. Probably her belly, her perfect inny belly button. Maybe lower.

I think how I'm no saint, how many times I've wanted to just fuck her, to fuck her out of this thing. On the couch, leaning over the kitchen table, in the backseat of a car. We used to when we first met, and I didn't want it then. She was the adventurous one. I was lazy, wanted it in bed, under the covers. Now that I can't have it, any of it, except for shower sex in a room that she can almost pretend is pristine, I dream of dirty fucking, of not washing first, of spitting on my hand and rubbing her raw. Sometimes, I'll see a woman with a sheen of sweat on her face or a bit of mud on her calf, and I'll ache in that way that starts in my balls and rides up through my chest.

I almost cheated once. Back when Cate was too embarrassed to tell me what was wrong, when I thought it was just that she couldn't stand to touch me. That old cliché—a woman in my office. Younger. Wanted to touch me. I nearly did. So close, just a yes away. A yes that I didn't say. And then, later, when Cate finally broke down and told me about the rituals, the germs, the losing her mind, I was so grateful for that one small no.

I would never tell Cate these things—maybe she already knows them, the way she knows about my hidden porn stash. I never used to care about porn, but now the back of the TV cabinet is filled with DVDs of women who go on their knees, who fuck with their backs against trees, who will touch each other without thought, and open their mouths and bodies to whoever and whatever might fit in. It's embarrassing to me, somehow, but somehow it also allows me to do this thing. To sit on a toilet seat in a hotel room waiting, hoping that my wife's internal demons will clam shut for an hour so I can hold her in my arms, so I can enter her and feel her clench around me.

Cate's nearly finished washing. It's in the sound of the water hitting her when she bends down to wash her calves, her ankles, the bottoms of her feet.

"Your turn," she calls. I step into the shower behind her, stunned as I always am by her body. I see it so rarely anymore. She's so pale and pink, so pure. Turned away from me, she's all hips and ass and the small muscles that grace her upper back. She scoots over to let me under the water, and her pink nipples are pointed. Water runs down her skin in rivers, big and small.

She doesn't touch me, but she watches while I wash. I go the same order—head, chest, belly. Carefully. The order is important. So is the way I hold the soap, the length of time that I rinse. The soap shouldn't touch any part of the body but my hands.

I lather my hand and run along the length of my hard cock. My teeth ache with how much I want her to touch me. But she just watches this too, her real smile, the one where she doesn't show any teeth, but instead just the laugh lines of her lips. I wash the rest of me and stack my soap on top of hers.

"All clean," I say.

She stands a minute, appraising. I stand under the spray and wait. This is the final checkpoint. If we can make it here, we're good. We're golden. I hold my breath.

Cate reaches out one finger, wipes it on my arm as though giving me the white glove test.

"Clean," she says. And she kisses me, uses her lips and tongue. Soapy taste and I wonder if she's taken to washing her mouth out again. I hope not.

I pull her toward me, not breaking the kiss. I know she hopes that if we do this enough, that if she touches me and I touch her and nothing bad happens, no one dies, then her mind will deem me—me and sex—safe. Clean.

We're wet and warm and completely clean and all I can think about is sex. My tongue in her mouth, across the front of her lips and down her throat. She's wet enough to drink. I touch her nipple, loving the way the water breaks across its point.

Her mouth is open, letting water in, letting breath out. She watches me touch her and there's no fear in her eyes. I'd almost forgotten how she looks when she moves past the alarm hour, back into her body.

She touches me, hands traveling the length of my arm, down my belly. My cock strains up toward her touch long before she gets there. Cate makes a cup with her hands and lets the water fall in. Then she cradles my cock: warm skin and water, the pressure of something beyond my own hand.

"I wish we had another bar of soap," she says. "I'd lather my hands and I'd jack you off like that."

My cock jumps under her fingers, sends its holler all the way up my body. I can feel her words in my shriveled fingers, in my waterlogged toes. I can feel her words in my grin that just won't stop. "I love it when you talk dirty," I say.

And then I dip my fingers into the wet space between her legs.

Cate says something, but I can't hear it over the sound of the water, over the sound of my veins running hot desire. My cock, impatient, insists against her belly.

"Wait," Cate says. "Wait." Her eyes are big and round. Drops of water hang from her lashes. I keep my fingers perfectly still inside her. Not a muscle, don't move. Her body shivers in the steam. She closes her eyes. I resist the urge to bend her over, force her into some kind of normalcy with my thrusts. I can't hate her. Not for this. And yet, my cock is pissed, a hard angry red.

Cate does her chipmunk cheeks again, counts from ten with her lips against her teeth. I start to take my fingers out, to resign myself to another week of bad porn and dirty thoughts.

She catches my wrist. "You're going to have to force me," she says.

"What?"

"I need you to just...If you don't, the clock's gonna go off and I'm going to run out that door screaming like a madwoman. And you, you'll be left with your..." She doesn't say it, but I know she's found the porn, that she's cried over it, talked about it with her therapist. I also know that it isn't the porn that made her cry, it's that she misses it too. The way it used to be. The way we used to be.

Who knew my heart and cock were attached this way, jumping at the same time, pulling on each other?

Still, I can't. "Honey," I say.

"And it wouldn't be just for a week," she says. "It's got to... you've got to make it stop. I'm afraid it won't stop."

My fingers are still inside her while she speaks. The warm walls of her body quiver my fingers with each breath. I try to focus on her words and the blue of her eyes. Are those tears, or shower?

"Did your therapist—?"

"Fuck my therapist," she says. "No, fuck me. Fuck me until that fucking voice shuts the fuck up."

All I can hear is fuckfuckfuck. It's like the cleaner Cate has to be, the dirtier her mouth gets. I take my fingers from her and turn her to face away from me. Her ass is red from the shower. So warm and heavy under my hands. I spread her cheeks apart, slide lengthwise between them. My cock is a perfect fit between her curves. Now, I just nestle in, like between a bun. We used to fuck like this; we'd warm up for hours, get her ready, and then she'd open her perfect ass to me. She'd let me into the dirtiest, sexiest parts of her.

I press myself against her, make her lean forward until she nearly falls over.

"Put your hands on the wall," I say.

She shakes her head no. "Dirty." Her voice is small as a child's.

I take her hands and press them to the shower stall. "It's clean," I say. "It's clean."

Her body shudders and shudders, but she doesn't take her hands down. I spread her legs as far as they'll go inside the tiled shower. My cock is so ready for her. It noses the wet of her skin, to the even wetter space between her legs.

I want to wait, but I can't. Dear god, I can't. I enter her. The slide in isn't slippery but stop-and-go with the water and how long it's been, but it's so perfect. The best fit. I don't give her a chance to relax, or to think about what's happening. It's when she starts thinking about it, loop-de-loop, that things go haywire. So I just fuck her, hard enough that the shower spray is in my face. Hard enough that my feet are sliding, hers are lifting, and we're both moving forward beneath the water.

"Oh, Jesus," she says. If my ear wasn't right next to her lips, I wouldn't even hear her. "Oh, fuck, Bobby." When was that last time she said my name like that?

And then, she does the most amazing thing. She puts her fingers in her mouth and then her hand moves down, down. I can tell by the crook of her elbow that she's actually touching herself. And it's the hottest, dirtiest thing I've ever fucking seen. I close my eyes, slow my strokes. I have to, or it's going to be over. And I want to wait for her, I want to help her get wherever it is she needs to go.

"You're so clean, baby," I say into her ear. "So. Fucking. Clean."

It sounds silly, but it sounds right too. It sounds even better when she moans and arches against me.

Her voice a hiss. "Keep fucking me," she says. "Keep—"

And I am. We are. But I won't come. Not yet. I need us to stay here for just a little longer: My cock sliding in and out of my wife. Her fingers touching something besides her elbow. The way she throws her head back and lets the water and air in and the sound out.

I need us to stay here as long as we can. Because this is the place we live for now, the rare, small moments between clock ticks. Suspended in time, when we can almost believe that everything is new and clean and sparkling with promise.

A ROOM AT
THE GRAND

Thomas S. Roche

He checked his tie nervously as he entered the lobby; he'd never gotten used to wearing the damn things, and it hung disheveled and half-undone at the too-tight collar of his white dress shirt. Even so, he was glad he'd worn it; dressed in a suit, he could walk through the lobby of a four-star hotel and, despite himself, not feel like an utter choad.

After a cursory nod to the bellman's greeting, he settled into a sumptuously velvet-lined antique chair, plucked his phone from his jacket pocket, and dialed.

"Hello?" she answered brightly.

"Hi. I'm here for our appointment," he said.

"Room fourteen-twenty-three," she said. "Fourteenth floor, left off the elevator, I'll leave the door ajar. See you in a few!"

She hung up. He took a deep breath, regarded his cell phone, the little image of her gracing the screen. He frowned, returned his phone to his jacket. As he stood, he looked at the bellman as if to say, "You lookin' at me?" but the guy hadn't even registered him, or if he had, he didn't care, and why should he? No question about it: everybody did something dirty in a hotel.

This was particularly true of the Beaumont Grand—not quite the nicest hotel in town (that honor went to the oddly named "Q"), but damned close, and quite possibly the snobbiest. Without expending too much mental effort, he tried to put his finger on it. First, you see, there's the anonymity. Antiques or no, smiling doorman or no, bell desk, patrons, whatever—these people could be doing *anything*. Second, and more importantly, there's the stink of *money*. The kind of person who could afford a room at the Beaumont Grand was supposed to be the sort of person who could *afford* to do anything. Rock stars, politicians, and high-profile businessmen might worry a bit about who'd see them heading upstairs with whom, but the Beaumont reeked of old money privilege and seemed to be populated by the kings of a distant age.

The reality, he pondered as he boarded the elevator, was probably quite different; these people, like Ali, bookmarked Expedia and hit HotWire at 3:00 A.M. on a Sunday when the brokers released their room blocks, then came here and did things they'd gloat about in their libidinous minds for years, possibly decades, to come.

He hit 14 and put his hand in his pocket.

As the doors closed, he took out the torn slip of paper. Cheap and glossy, it looked texture-wise like one of those ads from the back pages of *Hustler*, which it wasn't, and content-wise like one of those ads from the back page of the *Weekly*, which it also wasn't. It bore a photo of Allison looking exceedingly hot in a streetwalker costume from the Pimp & Ho ball—micromini, halter top, trashy plastic boots, bad earrings, and makeup that could have frightened small children. In addition to her name, mobile number, and prices for a half hour, one hour, and overnight, it bore a series of helpful bullet points:

- 32C-23-32 goth hottie
- Discrete
- Intimate
- Playful
- Speaks Greek

Two things rendered the advertisement either deceptively real or tellingly unreal: Allison had mistaken "discrete" for "discreet"—spelling, or more accurately usage, had never been Ali's strong suit—and after printing the ad out on, he suspected, the color laser at work, she'd taken the time to underline *Speaks Greek* three times, circle it, and put a star on either side of it. He thought it was a bit of overkill, but then, he was known to be slightly dense from time to time.

As if to reassure himself he'd gotten the date right, he lifted the ad and looked at what was stapled behind it: a page from his day planner, with *Grand Beaumont* scrawled in Allison's handwriting—*thirty minutes, 11-11:30 P.M., bring cash* written in small letters underneath, in case he was clueless about that, too.

The elevator bonged cheerfully; he exited, turned left, found room 1423 with the deadbolt shot to hold the door ajar. He pushed in and shut the door behind him.

The room was big enough to have a small entryway, but it was not a suite; there was no sitting area for him to cross before he saw her stretched on the bed, gloriously lit by bedside lamps and looking every bit the whore he was about to pay for.

"Hi," she said with a smile in her voice. "I'm Ali. Are you Scott?"

He opened his mouth to say "Yeah," but forgot the word somewhere halfway between his freshly polished wingtips and his inexpertly knotted necktie. It was not an easy word to forget, but he did it, his eyes surging from Ali's black stiletto all the way up the immaculate curve of one leg in its sheer black stocking, the calf turned just so to reveal the seam accentuating its shape, the thighs slightly spread to show the smooth flesh where black lace hitched to garters. There, his eyes and his brain fought a battle, because devouring Ali's legs had been so unspeakably pleasant that he almost didn't want to move on to the rest of her. He did, though, taking in the tiny slip of see-through fabric—thinner than the stockings, if anything—that formed her thong, then moving on to her glorious hips framed by her garter belt in addition to her tattoos, and her breasts crammed into an impossibly tight push-up bra that had her spilling out everywhere and looking like a D-cup at the very least.

Then there was her hair, cascading everywhere on the expensive white pillowcases. It was freshly black—it had been going chocolate-sepia the last few weeks—and her candy-apple-red lipstick made her lips stand out in the waterfall of black hair and pale, glorious face, face, face.

"You look...you're gorgeous," he murmured. "You're, uh, much hotter than your picture."

Her face brightened, the smile on her red mouth managing to look gullibly pleased and cynically lascivious. "Aww," she said. "What a *wonderful* thing to say, Scott. You're very cute yourself. Very much my type." Her voice was equal parts flirtation/seduction and I-am-blowing-smoke-up-your-ass. Something about that made him get hard immediately, which he had already been well on his way to.

Ali squirmed and wriggled on the bed, deliciously aware that he was watching her every move. She drew her hand down her front, absently, letting her thighs ease just far enough apart that when she began to toy with the slim elastic of her thong, he could see that she'd shaved for the occasion. "Now, Scott," she said, mock-seriously. "I like to get business out of the way up front." She said this as her hand slid down into her thong and obscured her already plainly visible sex; two fingers disappeared smoothly, and her eyes went fluttering a bit and rolling slightly back in her head while her red lips parted, puckered, relaxed, puckered as she uttered a surprised-sounding "Oh!" and then bit her lower lip with one white canine, as if trying not to moan uncontrollably.

It was a magnificent technique for not losing the sexual tension while she demanded money; in fact, it made him reach for the money so fast he almost couldn't figure out how to get his hand in his pocket.

"Of—of course," he said, finally getting the roll of bills out of his pocket and holding them out as he took a step closer.

She shook her head. "Uh-uh," she said softly, fingering herself. "Show me."

It took him a moment to get them fanned: five hundreds, the corners crisp and the portraits of dirty Ben Franklin leering obscenely.

Ali pouted a little while she continued to finger herself—two fingers, slowly in and out, rubbing her clit in between strokes in, her hips moving in time, and her red lips trembling. "You just want the half hour, then," she asked.

"Yeah, I thought—" He froze.

"We'll see," she sighed, working her two fingers deeper and spreading her legs a bit farther. "There's an ATM in the lobby." She laughed lightly. "Put them on the table," she said. "And take your clothes off, Scott. All of them."

He tried to do it all at once, and the bills ended up a crumpled pile rather than the neat fan she had probably envisioned. Standing next to the bed, he watched her as he started to undress. His coat was off swiftly; his eyes locked on hers as she squirmed in time with her fingers going into her pussy and caressing her clit. Next came his shoes, but when he went to undo his tie, she moved so fast he barely knew it was happening—her fingers were out of her and on his belt buckle, the other hand on his tie as she deftly rolled over and lowered her face into his crotch.

Now it was time for his eyes to roll back in his head, as he felt her leaving aggressive lipstick stains across his gray slacks; he thought maybe he should care, but he didn't. His zipper came down easily and his cock came free; her lips glided down, sucking eagerly as she gave out that unfamiliar little moan again, muffled now, and he kept fumbling with his buttons until they were all undone except the top one, since she was using his tie like a handle to keep him rocking back and forth against her as she sucked him. Her other hand slid his boxers down, and it all ended up at his ankles; he awkwardly stepped out of them, but it wasn't easy since Ali wouldn't let go of his cock. He let out a gasp.

He almost said it, but she knew before he did, coming up for air, panting and smiling over his glistening, lipstick-smeared cock. She nuzzled at his balls and looked up at him wickedly.

As he towered over her, panting, he noticed for the first time that her thong was put on over her garter belt, but he'd already decided that the slutty little garment wasn't coming off—why bother, when the slightest tug would pull it out of the way?

Then she was away, sliding back onto the enormous bed, spreading out widthwise across it, and licking her fingers like she just couldn't stop sucking.

"How do you want me, Scott?" Ali asked between messy slurps.

He'd gotten the tie, but he tore the top button; it went sailing away and he kicked off his socks as he mounted the bed, suddenly ravenous for her. Sure, it was all a game, but this kind of game was better than the real thing as far as he was concerned.

He went right for her, plucking the crotch of her thong out

of the way, and feeling the pulse of her heat as he found her smooth-shaved sex with his tongue. He spent a moment getting to know the immaculate lips as she gasped in surprise, slid his tongue tip in to taste her—mild and sweet, less tangy than other times, a soft taste of the way she was when she'd been very wet for a very long time. Then he made it to her clit and gently began working it, the taste of her mingling with the warmth against his tongue and the soft, slow bucking of her hips.

"Oh, that's how you like it," she purred, her voice hoarse. "Not even a kiss first. Mmmmmm…well, a different kind of kiss, at least…oh!"

She settled into the sensations, letting him suckle on her clit for a long, lush series of strokes as he brought his fingers up and began to tease her like he was going to finger-fuck her. She sounded close to coming, he thought; any minute now, he'd bring her off and she'd twist and pump against him and he'd feel like a pro himself. It turned out he was right about where she was—that became clear when she blurted out in the same inarticulate tone he had been about to use just before he came in her mouth. But then she got real articulate, sighing, "How do you want me, Scott?"

He remembered himself, licked and kissed his way up her body, popped one breast out of her too-tight bra and suckled it gently as the nipple hardened. Then he slid alongside her, turned her away from him and nestled behind her, his hard and sticky cock against her perfect ass.

"Your ad says you do Greek," he said.

"Like a native speaker," she purred, her whole body trembling slightly as she ground against him. He pulled away—fuck, doing that against him, she could make him come faster than with her mouth. "I fucking love it."

Breathing hard himself, aching to slide into her, he stepped back into character and said with savagely mock innocence: "It's included in the price?"

Her hand had already disappeared under the pillow and returned with a bottle of lube. She scowled over her shoulder at him and said, "No, asshole. I pay you. Now fuck me."

He chuckled and took hold of her hair, using the hand-hold to guide her onto her belly while he licked his way down her back. This she hadn't expected, and it pleased him somewhat to be able to surprise her. There was that thong again, so impossibly slutty that it turned him on anew as he plucked it out of the way to tongue the whore's asshole. He parted her cheeks and slid his tongue against her hole, and she let out a long series of mildly obscene comments, getting more devotedly blasphemous as his tongue swirled in circles and then gently wriggled its way into her; if that hadn't already coaxed enough dirty words out of Ali, his two fingers sliding easily into her extremely wet pussy would have—and he could feel from the way she bucked and trembled against him that there was not going to be a protest this time. Flipped on her stomach like that, Ali couldn't really pull away, not with her ass in the air and his fingers working deep inside her. She probably could have, but she didn't.

Ali didn't usually come twice, so he had to stop at the very last second, hating himself for not lubing up his cock. Still, the bottle was next to him on the bed, and in record time his fingers went from mildly slippery inside her pussy to extremely slippery inside her ass, and the wide-eyed yowl that came out of her made him worry for a second he had gone too fast. He hadn't; she pushed back onto his hand and moaned. He moved up on top of her until the position was just too awkward to keep his fingers inside her ass; by that time, he'd gotten his cock there and slicked it up with lube. It pressed easily against her entrance and he tangled his fingers in her hair as he penetrated her, not expecting the way she froze and stayed painfully, terrifyingly still—then pushed onto him and came, the intense spasms of her asshole unmistakable even though she wasn't making a sound for the first fifteen seconds. Then she was howling—screaming, almost—and surging up against him, trembling all over, this time not stopping when he sank deep inside her and felt her asshole clenching tight around his cock.

"Give me a minute," she whispered, and he went to pull back, and she shook her head violently, reaching back behind her to pull him harder onto her.

After a long slow series of breaths she began to rock against him, and she nodded, whimpering "Uh huh," every time he thrust, the plea growing louder every time he thrust faster.

He wanted to make his whore come again, but the way her perfect body moved under him was too much, as was the tight embrace of her around his cock. He went slack trying to stop it, then said, "Fuck it," actually said it aloud in a big breathy sigh, and came inside her ass with such intensity that he couldn't remember the last time he'd seen so many stars.

He attempted to pull out when he finished, but she had gotten hold of his wrist and tugged hard at it when he tried to withdraw. "Stay," she said. He did, and softened slowly over several long minutes as her ass clenched around him. The rhythmic sensation of her muscles embracing him made him start to get hard again. She could tell, too, feeling him swell inside her, which was apparently exactly what she wanted. When she had him halfway there, she reached under, put her hand down her thong, and rubbed herself rapidly until she came, almost silently—just a long low whimper as she felt her body giving in to it, verging on a sob.

The clenching of her muscles as she came finally squeezed

him out of her, and he remained there against her ass, half-hard, as she breathed deep.

When he slid off of her and relaxed into the bed, she rolled over, drawing her hand over his face, and looking at him with love in her eyes. He moved to kiss her and she pulled away.

"I'm afraid we've run over time, Scott," she said with a sad shake of her head. "I need to ask you for another five hundred dollars."

He opened his mouth, closed it, opened it, frowned, smiled.

Her long fingers went slowly down his chest and belly to his cock, which started to get hard as she took it in her hand, never breaking eye contact.

"There's an ATM in the lobby," she said with a flirty little smile.

He frowned at Ali and reached for his pants.

TROPICAL GROTTO, WINTER STORM

Teresa Noelle Roberts

A lan and I dreamed of a winter vacation someplace sunny
and secluded, with palm trees and white sand and bright
flowers and warm, clear water. And maybe parrots.

We fantasized to each other about making love under a tropical waterfall or in a coral lagoon. Hell, we'd have been happy
to frolic under the waterfall or snorkel in the lagoon, and then
make love in an ocean-view hotel room.

But a blown transmission ate a chunk of our vacation budget,
and the rest was covering our trip to a combined family reunion
and birthday party for Alan's ninety-year-old grandfather.

In suburban Massachusetts.

In cold, gray, grim February.

His grandfather was a great old coot, and making Grandpa
happy was worth the trip for Alan and thus for me—but it was
pretty far from the vacation of our dreams.

Which is why we decided to stay in a hotel in Massachusetts—at least we'd have room service and privacy and those

nice hotel beds that are so conducive to wild weasel sex.

And why, when my hotel search turned up one that boasted an indoor "tropical" water park, I squealed with unholy glee.

I called Alan over to the computer. "Looks like we can get our tropical vacation after all!"

"That's incredibly silly and tacky," Alan said, "and by silly and tacky I mean 'just what we'll need to recover from Aunt Fran and her death-by-good-taste.' "

"It's not Grand Cayman, but it could be fun."

We pictured ourselves, after a hard day of schmoozing relatives, donning our bathing suits to drink piña coladas while tubing down an indoor river, or shrieking like kids on the giant water slides. I smiled. He grinned. We both started laughing.

And the next thing I knew I was booking a "water park getaway package," complete with extra towels and complimentary swim goggles.

And that, plus room service, would have been enough to get us through Family Reunion Hell.

We'd reckoned without the nor'easter that veered off its predicted course to slam Massachusetts. The nor'easter that changed our mini-vacation from pleasant to wild and wet.

We woke on what was supposed to be the morning of the party to a white world and a frantic call from Alan's mother telling us to stay off the roads. The caterer had gotten into an accident on her way to pick up the shrimp, and Grandpa had refused to leave his house on the theory that dying in a car crash on the way to his own ninetieth birthday party would end up as a human interest story on Fox News, thus embarrassing the entire family. We made all the proper disappointed noises—but between the lousy weather and the fact that the reunion had sounded about as entertaining as a root canal in the first place, Alan and I were delighted to fuck like bunnies, fall back to sleep, and then wake up to fool around some more while we waited for our room-service breakfast.

Fortified by eighteen-dollar bacon and eggs, we ventured down to the water park, which we'd arrived too late to check out the night before. The idea of goofing around in warm water and enjoying a prenoon rum drink in the campy faux-tropical décor sounded even more appealing if we could watch a blizzard raging outside.

Bracing ourselves for shrieking kiddies, but ready to shriek like kids ourselves, we opened the door that led to the water park area and found...

Silence.

Okay, not quite silence. There was burbling water, and Jimmy Buffett pouring out of the speakers, and a faint undertone that I finally identified as the wind howling outside.

But no splashing. No screaming children or laughing adults. Just us and a college-age lifeguard poring over a chemistry textbook. "Thank god!" she exclaimed when she saw us enter. "I was starting to think I'd risked my neck getting here for nothing. All the kids' parties canceled, and I swear every other guest at the hotel is in that sales meeting in the conference center." She buried herself once more in her huge textbook.

The water park was bright and colorful, decorated with tropical flowers both real and fake and potted palms adorned with blatantly fake parrots. There was even a tiny beach of gleaming white sand, splashed by machine-generated waves. It was like a B-movie set of a tropical resort.

And it made me feel playful, both in childish ways and not-so-childish ones.

We splashed around like kids and smooched like adults in love. I'd barrel down the water slide, squealing with glee, and land in Alan's arms. I'd giggle like a kid and then rub myself against him so my nipples throbbed against my bikini top and his cock tented his trunks. We played tag in the pirate caverns and necked in out-of-the way corners until my suit was as wet from the inside as it was from the outside.

I wasn't sure if I wanted to dunk Alan or jump his bones—possibly both at once.

He made up my mind for me. "Want to go back to the room?" he finally asked. He ran his hands along the undersides of my breasts and down my sides as he spoke, missing all the directly naughty bits but making me shiver with anticipation. He stroked back up my torso. His thumbs grazed my nipples. It was quick, nothing that would have been obvious if the lifeguard had looked up from the joys of inorganic chemistry, but my nipples spiked and throbbed, and my clit picked up the calypso beat.

I was snatching up our towels to leave when I got a better idea.

"Remember that tropical waterfall fantasy?" I said. "I think this is as close as we'll get for a while." I grabbed his hand and led him into the Palm Grotto.

His eyes grew wide. He looked like he was going to protest for a second. Then he grinned and let me pull him into the warm, bubbling water.

An immense hot tub with a current, Palm Grotto was tucked away in a grove of palm trees—potted, of course, but real—and mostly out of sight of the oblivious lifeguard. A waterfall poured from some cleverly disguised spot in an upper story, cascading over sculpted faux rocks. They'd planted ferns and some kind of bright flowering plant in crevices next to the cascading stream. It was all a little too pretty to be real, but hell, so were some of the pictures I'd seen of Hawaii.

Despite the snow-covered skylight and the swirling mass of white visible through the grotto's glass brick walls, I could squint and pretend we were somewhere warm and romantic.

And very private.

Okay, it smelled more like a hotel swimming pool than a tropical paradise, but I was willing to overlook that.

Buoyed by the deep, luxuriously warm water, I bobbed into Alan's arms and pulled him close for a deep kiss, the kind that should by rights have brought the water to the boiling point. It brought *me* to the boiling point, at least, so my skin flamed as he ran his fingertips down my spine and my sex pulsed.

His fingertips kept gliding, tracing down my spine to my butt.

Under the cover of the water, they dipped inside my bikini bottom to cup my bare ass.

I pushed against him harder, pressing against what felt like steel. He stopped touching me gently, got a good grip on my asscheeks, then squeezed them sensually. Hot water caressed me, and the motion tugged on my pussy lips. Delicious languor filled me. The warm water and the tropical ambience, fake though it was, made me want to take my time.

A window-rattling gust of wind brought me back to reality.

If we were really in a secluded tropical grotto, I'd have gone for slow and sensual. But we were in a public place—a largely deserted one, but who knew when bored business travelers might sneak out of their conference to play? I upped the ante by snaking my hand inside the front of Alan's trunks.

"Lucky these are baggy," I chuckled. "Otherwise you might rip something." His cock, already swollen, jumped at my touch and throbbed in my hand as I stroked it.

He kissed me as if he wanted to devour me, groaning into my mouth as I circled his head with my fingertips, then stroked back down the shaft. With my other hand, I flicked at his nipple.

He found my clit and started to circle with the confidence that comes from knowing your partner well.

The first waves of sensation took me by surprise, and I nearly bit Alan's tongue, startled by my orgasm's speed and force. My mind boggled as my hips bucked and my sex clenched and I gripped Alan for all I was worth, one hand digging into his shoulder like a cat clinging to the drapes, the other squeezing his cock.

"I've got to have you," he whispered, nuzzling at my ear. "Back to the room or..." He glanced toward the waterfall.

"Reading my mind again!"

With a show of nonchalance, we half-bobbed, half-swam to the waterfall.

The water poured over us, warm and forceful, and that last touch was all it took to let me pretend I was on Jamaica or Grand Cayman or Hawaii, not in a hotel in Danvers, Massachusetts, during a winter storm. I closed my eyes and could almost feel the tropical heat, could almost smell the frangipani and hear the peeping of tree frogs.

Then Alan moved against me, and I opened my eyes to see his swim trunks land on one of the sculpted "rocks." I decided that a water park in a hotel in Danvers—or a trailer park in a pasture in Peoria, for that matter—was fine as long as he was fucking me in it.

My bikini bottoms followed his trunks.

Buoyed by the water, I wrapped one leg around his waist and positioned his cock right at my opening—just enough to tantalize us both. I rolled my hips as best I could.

I held his cock, rubbed it against my clit, against my hungry slit, torn between prolonging the anticipation and feeling him inside me.

"I can tell how wet you are," Alan said, "even in the water."

And then he pushed down on my hips, skewering me on his cock.

I barely stifled a happy scream as his hot length filled me and I twitched and clenched around him. It wasn't quite an orgasm, but pleasure radiated from my full pussy throughout my body and I could tell it wouldn't be long...

Once we figured out how to move. That took time—probably only a few seconds, but they were awkward, frustrating seconds. "Not the easiest position," I said.

"It'll do," he said through clenched teeth. "Try wrapping your other leg around me." I complied, and he pushed deeper into me. His hands clasped under my ass, moving me.

On dry land, it wouldn't have worked for long. Alan's strong, and I'm pretty small and limber, but we're not yogis or Cirque du Soleil performers, and I think you'd have to be that freakily fit to pull that off.

In chest-deep water, though, it worked well enough. Alan couldn't really thrust, but he moved me up and down, and I clenched my cunt muscles around him, and we kissed and kissed until the heat from the kisses flowed down to meet the heat rising from where our bodies joined. My body felt heavy with want, and then it felt light and buoyant, and then I bit down on Alan's shoulder as I came.

He might have followed me over the edge if, at that moment, we hadn't heard voices. Distant voices, thank goodness, but they were getting closer.

A few people must have decided that soaking in the Palm Grotto would be more fun than enduring more sales meetings. Can't say I blamed them, but their timing stank.

Alan hissed a curse and detangled. Reaching for his trunks, he said, "Race you to the room?"

I stated the obvious. "We're going to end up with a wet bed. Not that we care now, but we might later."

He threw the bikini bottom in my general direction, then

grinned and shrugged. "We'll just call housekeeping and make 'em wonder. That's the joy of being in a hotel."

G IS FOR GYPSY

Maxim Jakubowski

H e was a man who traveled a lot.

Which meant he used hotel rooms on almost all occasions.

If you'd asked him what his strongest memories were of foreign cities, he'd always remember the hotel, the room. Not the monuments or the museums or the architectural and cultural wonders of the place. But then he wasn't much of a tourist.

Every time he walked into a new room, shortly after arrival in a new town, he would sigh. He knew this particular home away from home for the next few days would prove both exhilarating in its potential for sex or eroticism, or just damn lonely if, yet again, he was to inhabit it alone for the duration.

Sex and loneliness. Two feelings that invariably went hand in hand.

"Here are the keys," the uniformed young woman at reception said, handing him back his passport and a small folded paper wallet with keys and breakfast time information. "We've given you room four-eleven."

It would be room 411. Out of all the hotel rooms in the world, what were the odds of being given room 411 again?

"Just my luck," he sighed, as his heart dropped or stomach sunk or whatever could best describe his body's reaction to the news. A feeling of sudden vertigo, of drowning in a sea with no water.

"Is the hotel full?"

Maybe he could ask to be moved into another room?

"Yes, sir," the receptionist looked up. "It always is at festival time."

"Okay."

The elevator.

The long, endless corridor, which had always reminded him of *Barton Fink,* the movie, albeit in more opulent ways. Or the Overlook in Kubrick's film of *The Shining.*

The door.

The key in the lock.

The light.

The room.

The bed...

He dropped his luggage to the carpeted floor. Opened the window slightly to let some air in and lowered the heat level on the thermostat.

He sat himself on a corner of the bed. Closed his eyes. Opened them again. It made no difference. He could still see the long silhouette of her pale body spread across the double bed, her legs apart, her slight breasts barely hillocks amongst the blinding, white landscape of her torso as she lay on her back and earth's gravity pummeled them down to almost nonexistence, the soft brown pinkness of her nipples like two minuscule beacons in the sea of flesh. The billion ebony dark curls in her hair washing over the sheets. The way the sun on a summer day past had caressed her dormant skin as its rays whispered their way through the open windows and caressed her nakedness.

It was as if she were still here.

Or maybe it was the ghost of her, following him along from country to country, from hotel room to hotel room, like a Flying Dutchman's curse as he sought to escape her memory. But he knew inside he never would. You don't forget the unforgettable.

His brain cells, out of control, now began to focus on all the sharper details of her anatomy, the angles, the curves, the indelible memories of her softness, the smell of her breath, the whiteness of her teeth, the longing and thousand questions ever present in her eyes, and it was like yet another stab wound piercing both his heart and his gut in one swift decisive movement.

Tears welled up inside him. He loosened his belt and pulled his trousers down to his waist, and his fingers took hold of his half-hard cock and began caressing its velvety mushroom tip, arousing himself, allowing all those lost images of her to inspire him, to stimulate him. Had she not one day revealed that waiting for him to arrive from the airport in another hotel room in another southern city she'd been unable to suppress her urgent need for him, and had eagerly masturbated herself to a thunderous climax even though she knew they would be reunited just a couple of hours later following his own flight's arrival?

But today he could not achieve sufficient hardness, and soon gave up.

It was as if the hotel room itself were alive and whispering to him on the sly that he would never know her again in the physical sense and there was no point jerking himself away to her memory, to her spirit, but then, the room suggested in his ear that there were other options, weren't there?

Pulling his black trousers back up to his waist and tightening the belt, he moved over to the traveling bag in which he kept his laptop and took the computer out of its protective sheath.

He opened the lid and booted up, then scoured the familiar chatrooms in search of sex.

There were some possibilities but after a few lines of dialogue with various other seekers of NSA activities, he realized there would be too much work, explanations, and lies involved to convince anyone to actually meet quickly enough, let alone do the deed. Unless he moved on to the gay or bi rooms, which on this occasion he was not yet in the mood for. Or desperate enough for.

He checked his mail. Mostly spam and the customary offers of cheap Viagra, Levitra, or no money back penis- and breast-enhancing products.

He undressed.

Looked at himself in the bathroom mirror. Wished he looked better, slimmer, younger, less morose.

Back in the room, he balanced the laptop on his knees and began writing her a letter.

Dear G.

I miss you. Terribly.

I know I have no doubt written this many times before, but you have left a hole inside of me. A deep, hollow cavern full to the brim with love and longing and despair.

You no longer even answer my messages and ignore me as if I were dead, but I don't mind. Writing to you in this way—which you probably find either despicable or pitiful—keeps you alive in strange ways. I can't let go of you, I just can't. Sorry.

I miss you. I hope you are happy, even if it is others who are now pleasing you, touching you, making your heart flutter somewhere, far away from here and me, which I foolishly, mistakenly still believe is where you should really be.

I'm in X. It's festival time again. You won't believe this, but I am in the very same hotel room. Room 411. Remember: I didn't ask for it. Maybe the hotel staff had a record of me being in the room before or it was sheer coincidence or again the booking computer proving mischievous.

Being here evokes such strange feelings, G.

Little since you has ever been the same. I am now nothing without you, but you have made me a better man. A man who knows what love is, can be. No woman had ever given herself to me so freely, without reservations, so wildly, and made me realize the terrible strength of love unleashed, as you did.

From that first, sometimes hesitant evening in room 411. Unveiling the beauty of your body, inch by inch, touching the paradise of your small breasts with my rough, undeserving touch, silent in awe at the perfect delicacy of the combined shades of pink of your nipples (which I had somehow expected to be much darker), slipping my fingers inside you, experiencing the divine heat of your cunt, spreading your wetness across my hand, and learning the musky, hypnotic smell of you, finger-tips traveling slowly through the mass of your pubic curls then moving into more dangerous territory toward your rear hole. And the worried, "No, not there, please..."

"Why?"

"Just not there, please."

That first night we did not even fuck.

Once stripped, we caressed each other, hardy explorers of newfound lands, we cuddled, we merged, we embraced rather frantically, skin against skin, lips against lips, sweat against sweat. You rode me repeatedly, like a young stallion. Dry-humping me like no one had ever done before. Rubbing your cunt and protruding bone against my hard cock, until I was even hurting but would never ask you to stop. I thought you would tear my cock skin away in the savage assault of your passion, while all the time I tried not to come, as if ejaculating on you would have been a crime, a sad admission of my innate vulgarity.

We writhed that way all night, between torrents of words, endless stories of our respective pasts, and inevitable questions about what might lie in our future. From the very first mail, months before, we knew this could only be an impossible love. But then it was also more than just animal attraction. We were so wrong for each other: ages, geography, past, activities, personalities. But, on the other hand, we were also so supremely right, weren't we? Remember how when apart we were almost telepathically in touch, always knowing when the other was about to call or do something particular. Emails crisscrossed the Web with mighty abandon; SMS messages littered the airwaves.

But mostly we were creatures who lived in hotel rooms, as we could not be seen publicly by others, irrespective of the foreign cities we traveled to.

I told you stories about the women who came before, the other hotel rooms I had lived in, seen. How, when once staying at the Algonquin in New York one night I had been kept up until the small hours of morning by acute sounds of pleasure from a woman in the room on the other side of the thin wall, who kept on achieving incredible orgasms one after another for hours on end. Never had I heard a woman so vocal in the throes of sex: moans, loud sighs, cries, shouts, rumblings, she went through them all, time after time. The bed in the opposing Algonquin room would bang repeatedly with every new thrust of her lover inside her against our common wall, and the anonymous woman would shriek, purr, scream; it was primeval, basic, awesome. And arousing: I must have come myself at least three times during the night, manually, provoked by the hurricane-like waves of pure sex streaming through from the other room. It was unavoidable. All I had to do was close my eyes, imagine the reverse image of the room I was staying in, and myself fucking her in every conceivable position of the *Kama Sutra*, with every variation evincing a new kind of sound from her throat. To say she was both loud and enjoying herself is something of an understatement. I even imagined that no man was capable of extracting such sounds of pleasure from a woman alone and that it was a procession of men entering the room and taking turns with her as she lay there with her legs splayed open and her apertures moist and slick and ripe for plundering at every turn.

Toward four in the morning, I finally managed to get some sleep.

The next day, I had to leave the hotel shortly after breakfast to go to a business meeting downtown and just as I exited my Algonquin room, the door to the next room opened and a woman exited. I had imagined the creature being so royally fucked in countless, alluring incarnations: sleek, blonde, redhead, brunette, tall, dusky, pale, opulent and skinny, beautiful and mysterious, but none of the visions I had evoked throughout the night corresponded with the reality!

She was a tiny little Chinese woman in her midfifties, with a wrinkled face and a shapeless body over which she had draped a faded brown fur coat which had known better days. She looked up at me, and her face betrayed no feelings of recognition or any embarrassment at having likely been overheard in the demented throes of her sexual exertions by a neighbor.

We both walked toward the elevator in silence and went our own ways forever.

I wonder, G., whether others ever heard us and tried to

imagine what we looked like, or with less obvious difficulty, what we were doing?

Not that we would have cared.

After we had technically become lovers at last, your own appetite and curiosity for the pleasures of the flesh knew no bounds, surprising even me, as you wanted this whole new world and wanted it now. Within a day, we were taking baths together with no shame. By the end of the first hotel room episode, that taboo word *love* was already leaking freely from our hearts.

We quickly became experts at living in a world of our own, a world within the existing world of rules and conventions, rules which we openly flouted, oblivious to the eyes of others.

Like the smiling leers of the men at the front desk of the hotel in Barcelona as they saw us pick up our key and walk arm in arm toward the elevator, noticing the disparity in our ages and looks, and guessing all too well the boundless fornication we were about to embark upon. In that room, in the shadow of Gaudi's Parc Guell, where we fucked mercilessly, leaving blood all over the sheets as your period caught us in ambush but never slowed our frantic ardor.

The breakfast room at the Washington Square Hotel in New York, where the Filipino waiter imprudently (or was it unprofessionally) remarked how much my daughter looked happy. The only time I saw you blush.

A bathroom in a hotel in Port Sitges where my sense of transgression knew no bounds, and I burst in on you sitting peeing and harvested your hot stream in the cup of my hands, a sensation of heat that has marked me forever and which I have craved after ever since, not just on my hands but all over my body in my desperation to capture the sheer essence of you.

Was it Paris, New York, Calcata, Washington D.C., or somewhere else where I hastily withdrew my cock from inside you and came too early, my white seed pearls like beautiful stains across the thick jungle surrounding your cunt lips? A mishap that gave us a damn scare as you feared a most inopportune pregnancy, and all future fucks had to be lessened with a condom.

"Oh, how you fill me," you would say.

"Oh, how I want you," I would say.

Oh, how my heart would break into a thousand shards every time I took you from behind and enjoyed the incomparable sight of my dark cock stretching your pink lips and burying itself deep inside you while the eyelet of your ass would almost wink at me, as if inviting further depredations. And the obscene thought that one day other men would see you thus, would contemplate the tragic pornography of your indecency, was enough to make me cry.

But I did not have the right to ask you to be mine and mine only. I was scared to do so. Not because it would have been wrong; it would have been. But because I was in fear of your answer. Knowing your awful pride and will for independence. Later I realized that there were actually days and nights when you would have wanted me to do so and offer a more permanent form of commitment. Become genuine girlfriend and boyfriend, whatever that meant or entailed. Move to the city where you lived so we could see more of each other or you might be able to call me at any time of day to meet up, however innocently, for a coffee and a chat.

Why is it that love grows at different speeds between people who care for each other, need each other badly? Not fair, eh…

Many hotel rooms later, you finally left me. You wanted to live your life. You wanted other adventures. From the very first night, you had told me you were a gypsy and that you would not allow any man to catch you, imprison you. Let alone me.

An urban gypsy flitting through the lives of men, destroying hearts and souls with cheery insouciance, a falling star amongst us mortals. Oh, how you burned me.

Where are you now, embarking on what beautiful adventures with witty and sexy strangers, witnessing vistas I know nothing of? The last time we spoke, you would no longer even tell me of your plans because you guessed right: whatever news you provided me with would be betrayed by me one day, used in a story somewhere as some exotic fictional character that only you and I would recognize. You did not want to be a character in a book, G. Forgive me. But then all I wanted you to be was a lasting character in my life. Fiction is only second best, you know, a consolation for the unworthy.

I still want you badly.

The warmth of your mouth around my pulsing cock.

Your fingers weighing my swollen balls, learning how a man is constructed at his most intimate.

The generosity of your eyes.

The foolishness of your wonderful youth.

The ghostly pallor of your body in a hotel room where we have just made love. The flowers in your hair when you accompany me to an official function and are proud to say, "This is my man."

So, here I sit in room 411 of the Palace Hotel. I am naked. I am pitiful. I am lonely. Hotel rooms remind me of sex, of you.

Oh, just to hear the sound of your voice.

You belong here.

I send you this forlorn kiss.

He pressed SEND and the email made its way to wherever she would pick it up, if she ever did. He expected no answer, of course. That would be asking for too much. Things were clear cut and he would never see her again. Maybe he would occasionally hear about her through third parties, but then even that was unlikely. Different countries, languages, ambitions.

He sighed.

Washed his face with cold water and slipped on the white terry-cloth bathrobe and returned to the computer.

The emptiness weighed on him. Once again, he clicked his way into a chatroom.

A sharp sense of unworthiness settled on his mind.

As if he finally realized that he had done G. wrong.

Guilt was a dangerous thing.

It calls for punishment.

Oh, yes.

There was a discreet knock on the door. He walked across, still wearing the bathrobe. Outside the hotel room windows, night was falling and the sound of distant sirens—police? ambulance? firemen?—echoed through the city as it pursued its descent into darkness. He opened the door.

The stranger looked even larger than the photo he had posted online and forwarded to him during the course of their conversation and ensuing negotiation.

A swarthy guy, gym sharpened and feral.

"You 'slave of G?' " the man asked.

"Yes," he lowered his eyes submissively. It was the handle he had used online.

"Good," the man said, taking a decisive two steps into the room. He looked him up and down, maybe checking that the few details he had revealed during their chatroom conversation and then over the telephone were correct. He appeared satisfied and slammed the door shut behind him.

The point of no return had been crossed.

"So, this what you want? You're sure? No going back now?" the visitor asked.

"Yes," he meekly answered. Fear was now turning to resignation.

"Yes, sir," the man ordered sharply.

"Yes, sir," he said meekly.

"Better."

The taller man approached him and forced him to take a few steps back into the room, until he stood by the bed. The visitor lowered his hands and took the bathrobe belt and undid it, then quickly pulled the garment off him.

He stood naked.

Again, the visitor looked him up and down. And smirked.

He had already obeyed the initial instructions he had been provided with once the assignment had been arranged. He was fully bare, having shaven all the hair around his cock and balls while the stranger was en route to the hotel. He shivered briefly.

"Nice cunt, looks clean," the man remarked.

"Thank you, sir," he answered obediently. The act of shaving down there had made him feel even more naked, available, ripe for all sorts of humiliation.

"On your knees, slave."

He did so.

The man untied his trousers and exposed himself, presenting a thick, half-hard cock to the kneeling, naked host.

"Open wide," he said.

He took the semitumescent cock inside his mouth, where it hardened like rock within a few seconds, thrusting hard against the back of his throat, as he tried not to choke. The man took violent hold of his hair and conducted his movements with brutal, metronomic regularity.

The cock had an acrid taste and its texture was surprisingly spongy, which he had not expected. As he mechanically continued sucking the stranger's member, the room surrounding him seemed to murmur to him, "See, now you know what it felt for her to take your cock into her mouth...now you know what it feels to be a woman..."

There was another gentle knock on the door.

The visitor pulled his cock out of his drying mouth.

"Who is it?" he asked.

Catching his breath, he said, "Another guy I spoke to in the chatroom. I wasn't sure whether either of you would actually show up. You know how it is with chatroom meets. I reckoned if I made two appointments, there was a better chance one of you at least would show up. We don't have to open the door, if you don't want to."

The other man smiled, cock still at full mast.

"Why not? The more the merrier. Let him in."

He rose from the floor and went over to the door and opened it. The new visitor was a wiry Chinese guy. His gaze greedily focused on his bare cock. The earlier stranger walked over and explained the situation, offering the Asian man the opportunity to withdraw, should he wish to do so.

The new visitor seemed to enjoy the possibilities of the new situation and elected to stay.

"A greedy slave, indeed," one of the men remarked.

They both undressed.

The Chinese man lay on the edge of the bed, offering his uncut but already unsheathed erect cock, and the larger of his two visitors took hold of their newfound slave by the scruff of his neck and pushed him down to his knees again.

"Suck him," he ordered.

The new cock was thinner, veiny, and tasted differently. He

diligently set to work, already mentally comparing the experiences.

As he did so, the first visitor to the room sharply took hold of his soft cock and balls and, pulling both backward and slightly upright, forced him into the right position he required. He spat on his raised rump and with two fingers lathered the abundant saliva around his anal opening, testing his elasticity and resistance.

"Nice and tight," he remarked. "That's how I like my slaves." He suddenly slapped the slave's arsecheeks and then violently thrust himself inside him, breaching the ring of flesh in one single movement.

He couldn't help himself from screaming. It burned like hell as the alien penis buried itself deep inside his innards. But he still managed to keep on sucking the cock now fucking his mouth.

"Good boy, good boy," the Asian man said.

Later, the two men changed places and used him thoroughly in all his available holes.

His mouth was dry and the muscles in his cheeks hurt, come dripped from his well-stretched opening and inside it felt like the fires of hell still, and as the men dressed in silence he lay on the bed, exhausted, willingly degraded as he had wished. He briefly imagined the strangers keeping him in slavery together, abducting him from this luxury hotel room, putting a black, studded leather collar around his neck, and transporting him still naked under a coat to another seedy hotel room which would smell of piss and shit and stale tobacco, where he would be offered to all comers—fucked, whipped, beaten, peed on, and hosed like an animal.

But they just walked out, closing the door to room 411 behind them in continued silence.

Maybe it was a form of penance, he imagined.

Or more likely just more self-pity.

Oh G., he wrote inside his head, *this is what I now am without you, a lost soul, a creature of sex of loneliness. A man who travels a lot and gets up to abominable things within the sacred secrecy of hotel rooms. Without you.*

Just another letter he would never send.

REUNION

Lisabet Sarai

Three years since I last saw him, and now his plane is late. I perch on the edge of the chair across from the American Airlines desk where he told me to meet him, tension winding me tighter with every moment.

It's always like this. My chest aches. It's difficult to breathe. My nipples are as taut and swollen as if he already had them wrapped in elastic bands. I try not to be distracted by the stickiness between my bare thighs. I glance at the arrivals screen. His flight has just landed. Ten minutes, fifteen at most, before I can expect him. I fill my lungs deliberately and try to slow my racing pulse.

I hover between joy and terror. It has been so long, too long. What will he think of me, the strands of gray in my hair, the new wrinkles? What will he ask of me? Will I be able to give him what he needs? I remember other reunions, too few, too short. No time for more than a few kisses, a few playful swats on my bared butt. I remember lying on his lap in Golden Gate Park, my skirt flipped up around my waist. I can precisely recreate my shame and my excitement. I recall slouching down in the front seat of his car in a dark, sweltering parking garage, while he unbuttoned my blouse and dabbled his fingers in my cunt, naming me as his slut. A few hours every few years is all we manage, a country and my marriage separating us even as our history and our fantasies draw us together.

Today will be different. I've booked us a hotel room, in this city where neither of us live. We have the entire day. My husband waits for me at home, while I wait here in the airport for my master.

I don't call him that to his face. He'd mock me, his voice bitter. "If I were your master, I'd simply order to you leave him and come to me, and you would." He doesn't give me that order, although I suspect that he's tempted. He refrains, out of respect for me and my choices, or maybe in fear that his power over me is not as great as he would like to imagine. He spares us both, and I'm grateful, though now, waiting, burning to see him again, I almost wish that he'd put me to that ultimate test and take away the awful yearning that I feel when we're apart.

Every one of my senses is on alert, yet he manages to surprise me. I'm looking toward the gates. He comes from the other direction and calls to me softly. "Sarah."

I start and then laugh nervously. When I stand up, my bag tumbles off my lap to the floor, toys clattering inside. "You're here!" I feel clumsy, silly, stupid, but when he bends to kiss me, everything but the joy disappears. I'm flooded with it, gasping, overwhelmed.

In his limbs I feel his pitiless strength. His lips, though, are gentle, questioning. Am I still his? I melt, open my mouth and my mind to him. Does he sense the answer? Sometimes I am certain that he reads my thoughts. He laughs ironically and calls me suggestible. I don't know what to believe, which suits him perfectly. He wants me a bit off-balance.

I struggle to act normal, as if I were just meeting an old friend. "How was your flight? Did you have trouble with your connections? What about your baggage? Is that the only jacket you have? October here can be kind of chilly…"

"Hush," he says, laying a blunt finger upon my lips. "Don't chatter. Take me to the hotel."

We take public transit to the city center. The desk clerk eyes us curiously when we register, an odd couple, me so petite and my master so tall, checking into a hotel room at ten-thirty in the morning. I blush as the clerk hands back my credit card. "Have a nice stay," he says, and I'm sure that I catch something conspiratorial in his tone. However, my master is already pulling me toward the elevator; I don't have time to worry about what other people think.

This hotel is more than a hundred years old. I selected it deliberately, hoping that it might offer some Victorian style, but the room is fairly ordinary—no four-poster bed, no fireplace, no curtain fastenings that might serve double duty as attachment points for bonds.

There is, however, a fine wingback chair next to the window, with a footstool. My master tosses his backpack in the corner and settles himself into the chair. He grins at me, and butterflies swoop through my stomach. "Well, Sarah. Alone at last."

I stand on the other side of the room, the bed between us, clutching my bag. What I really want to do is to rush over and kneel at his feet. I can't move, though. It seems as though I'm in a dream, rooted to the spot. Hardly surprising. I've dreamed about this meeting for months.

How shall we start, then? Should I strip? The last time we

were in a hotel room together, years ago, he bound me to the desk chair with my stockings. The time before, he unscrewed the post from the fake colonial bed and fucked me with it until my screams brought the hotel management knocking on the door. But that was in another life, before I misread my master's heart and chose a different partner.

"So, what do you have in your bag?" he asks finally, after watching me squirm for long moments.

"I have the corset." I'd purchased it for myself, thinking to please him, knowing that there was no way he would ever buy me one.

"Good. And the other things that I told you to bring?"

"I have the ruler, the rope, the alligator clips, and the timer." I remove the items one by one, arraying them on the bed for his inspection. Without announcing it, I take out a package of condoms and place it on the bedside table. His eyebrows arch in a silent question, but he just nods.

"I'm sorry, but I couldn't find a rug beater, or the switches. It's too late in the year; the trees are too brittle. Anyway, I wouldn't have been able to carry them..."

"No excuses!" He sounds stern but I can see a smile twitching at the corner of his full lips. "I'm sure that you know better than to disobey me. We'll see about your punishment later."

He settles back in the chair, crossing one leg over the other. "Right now, I want to see you in your corset."

I carefully extract the gorgeous black satin garment from its tissue paper wrapping. My master looks relaxed, but I know he's not missing any detail as I pull my jersey over my head and attack the buttons at my waist. Of course I'm not wearing a bra. My nipples feel hot, as if illuminated by a spotlight. They seem to scream, "Look at me, see how stiff I am."

My rayon skirt pools around my ankles, and then I'm naked

in front of him for the first time in nearly two decades. His eyes widen but he doesn't say a word.

"Why don't you close your eyes while I put it on? It's rather an awkward process. And I want you to get the full effect."

"You can't hide anything from me, Sarah," he says, but still, he turns to look out the window while I struggle with the clasps and laces.

My fingers don't work at all, I'm so nervous. I know he's getting impatient, yet I can't seem to reach the last hooks. I suck in my stomach, worried that I've gained weight and I won't be able to fasten the thing, but finally, I manage.

The boned curves press into my flesh. I move a bit stiffly, my breathing shallow so that I don't burst open the hooks. The corset elevates and separates my breasts; they spill lushly over the top of the garment. Meanwhile, I can feel my bare buttocks bulbing out behind.

"Okay—I'm ready."

My master leans forward, eager, his smile baring sharp white teeth. "Very nice. Come over here."

Stumbling a bit in my high heels, I circle the bed and stand in front of him.

"Very nice indeed. Walk around for me, Sarah. Let's see more of your tits and your ass."

His mocking, lecherous tone thrills me. I'm terribly embarrassed, but I love showing off for him, and he knows it. My pussy swells and moistens. My nipples harden further, so painfully sensitive that one touch might send me into orgasm. He doesn't touch me, though. He just watches, while I strut back and forth in front of him, swinging my hips.

I notice the seaweed scent, rising from between my dampened thighs. I'm close enough to him to know he can smell it too. I don't dare to look at his face. Instead I hold my head high as he taught me, imagining that I'm wearing the collar he once promised me.

I feel his hot eyes ranging over my body, and I rejoice, knowing that I please him, that he's as aroused as I am. And all at once I'm awed by the power of our complementary fantasies. I want him to watch me; he has flown three thousand miles to do just that. He nourishes all my perverse notions, rewarding me for being the outrageous slut that I secretly am, the submissive, devoted wanton that he recognized in me, long years ago.

"Bend over," he says, his voice gruff with lust. I know exactly what he wants. I stand with my back to him, between the chair and the ottoman. I bend at the waist, presenting my ass to his gaze, holding the stool for support. He leans closer, but for a long time he still doesn't touch me.

His gaze traces paths across my bare skin. I swear I can tell when his eyes linger on the pale globes, or probe more deeply into the shadows between them. This inspection excites me beyond belief. I know that he'll touch me, sooner or later. I think that I'll die if he doesn't do it soon.

Still, I'm not prepared when he slaps one cheek with his open palm. "Ow!"

"You are such a nasty little girl! I had forgotten. But now I remember"—slap—"just how kinky and twisted you really are." He gives me three more spanks in quick succession, and I'm wailing out loud. At the same time, I'm hoping that he doesn't stop.

Of course he does, knowing how to stoke my fires with frustration, but only for a moment. "Across my knees, Sarah." The armchair is perfect for a spanking, and once again my spirit soars, as he lays into me, landing one ferocious blow after another on my tender butt. I'm where I belong, and both of us know it.

My butt is burning like it's been barbecued. It's starting to hurt enough to interfere with the pleasure. I wonder if he still has that uncanny sense of my limits that he used to demonstrate. Just as the thought crosses my mind, he whispers in my ear.

"I'll bet anything that you're soaking wet, Sarah." Without waiting for a reply, he thrusts three fat fingers deep into me. The fires race from my ass to my cunt and back. I come hard, grinding down on his hand, wanting him deeper, always deeper.

Afterward, he strokes my hair and plants little kisses on my ravaged ass. As for me, I'm content to just lie across his lap, glowing inside and out from his attentions. His erection pokes through his slacks and into my belly. He doesn't make any moves to release his cock, and I don't dare do so myself.

He's restless, though, aware as I am of the minutes ticking away. "Go get the ruler," he tells me. It amuses him to have me supply the instruments of my own torment.

"Oh, no, please, I'm too sore! Please, wait a while till I recover."

He ruffles my hair. "Okay, the rope then. Then I want you on your back on the bed. Legs wide, knees up to your shoulders."

I'm not sure that I'm still flexible enough to comply with his orders, but I manage. He loops the soft cotton rope around one thigh. "Sit up." I struggle to raise my back off the bed, and he slips the rope underneath, around my torso, then winds it around my other thigh. I'm now roped open, my cunt lips spread wide. It's an incredibly vulnerable position. I love it.

"Grab your ankles." When I do, he circles my wrist and ankle on the left and then the right, binding them together on each side. He finishes up on my left side with a neat bow.

His light mood has fled. He's concentrating, serious. A sparkle of fear dazzles me. What will he do, now that I'm totally helpless?

"How's that? Any pain, or numbness?" I wiggle my fingers and toes, then shake my head.

"Good. Now take a look at yourself."

I hadn't realized that there was a mirror at the foot of the bed. It's difficult to raise my head enough to regard my reflection, but it's worth it. In all the filthy pictures and videos he has sent me, I've rarely seen something so obscene. My thighs and belly are pale as marble contrasted with the black satin of the corset. My labia, emerging from the damp tangle of my pubic hair, are purple and puffy. They are stretched wide, open, and I can see a wet cavern between them, pulsing and quivering. I can't see my clit, but I can feel it, hard, insistent, crying out for his attention.

He zips open his backpack and pulls out a plastic bag. "I thought I should bring some supplies of my own." What does he have, I wonder, simultaneously worried and aroused. He replies as if I'd asked the question aloud. "Just a few clothespins and elastic bands." He hovers over me, searching my face. "Are you ready?"

I nod, then yell as he fastens a plastic clothespin to one of my pussy lips. It bites into my flesh. Sharp pain ricochets through my sex. Each echo modulates subtly in the direction of pleasure. I feel liquid trickling from my cleft onto the bedspread. Then he ramps up the pain again by clipping a symmetrical pin opposite the first.

"You know I'm a frugal guy. Why bother paying for toys when there are so many ordinary household items that can be pressed into kinky service? Shall I add a third clothespin on your clit, Sarah?"

The pain is already overwhelming, though muddied with pleasure. He's giving me the chance to choose. I don't really want more pain, but I want, I *need* to please him. There's so much time to make up for.

"If you want," I whisper. "Whatever you want." My clit

throbs, trembles, anticipating new agony. But I'm so aroused by now that the third pin hardly hurts. It just turns up the volume on the pleasure.

My master sweeps a fingertip through the opened folds of flesh in front of him, ending with a flick to the plastic pin fastened to my core. I moan and writhe, though I can hardly move, trussed up as I am. "You looks so sexy, Sarah. I've got to get some pictures."

He leaves me stranded on the bed, open and aching, while he gets his camera. The shutter clicks quietly as he captures me from a variety of angles. "These will keep me company, after you've gone." I'm so embarrassed I think that I'll die, but at the same I can't wait to see the photos. "Maybe I'll put these up on the Internet."

"No, you wouldn't..."

"Are you sure?" I'm not, not a hundred percent. He has a contrary streak that's a bit scary. "Or maybe I should email them to *him*." My master has actually met my husband, briefly, but he refuses to say David's name.

"No, don't, please..." David knows, intellectually, that I'm interested in BDSM, but I think he'd find these photos, this reality, pretty difficult to face.

My master leans over and brushes his lips across mine. "Don't worry. I think I want to keep these treasures all to myself." This brief intimacy is enough to set me shuddering, teetering on the edge of another orgasm. He sees, and laughs.

"Don't come yet, little one. I've got some new sensations for you."

He kneels on the bed between my splayed thighs, and I hope against hope that he'll simply pull out his cock and fuck me. But instead he grabs one of the elastic bands and starts snapping it hard against my inner thighs. The rubber stings the tender skin there; I notice that dampness seems to make the sensation stronger. The pain is not extreme, but it wakens the bite of the clothespins.

"The elastic leaves little red marks," he tells me. "I'll bet you'll still have them tomorrow."

There is no tomorrow. There is only now. I'm tingling all over, balanced between pleasure and pain, wanting him as I've never wanted anything else.

"Please..." I moan. "Please, Eric, touch me."

"Poor little Sarah," he says. "My poor horny little slave." He wriggles one of the clothespins on my labia, and I scream at the fresh rush of pain. He pulls roughly at the one attached to my clit. I tumble into a loud, frenzied climax, my body jerking like a helpless puppet as jolt after jolt of ecstasy hits me.

I regain my senses. I'm drenched with sweat. The bedspread underneath me is sodden. My master is smiling at me, looking pleased with himself. Love surges in me; tears tickle the corners of my eyes. I want to let him know what he does to me, how much I need him, how grateful I am.

"Feeling better now?"

I nod weakly. "Thank you..." The words I want to say suddenly seem silly, mushy. He'll just mock me the way he so often does. I lie silent as he removes the clothespins. I still feel the ghost of their bite. He begins to untie me, then stops.

"I'm hungry. How about some lunch?"

Maybe lunch would be a good idea, a chance to take a few deep breaths, reduce the intensity. "There's a nice sushi place around the corner that we used to go to..." I tend to avoid using David's name under these circumstances, too.

"Oh, I don't want to waste our time by going out. I'll just order room service."

"But..." He withers my objections with a masterful look.

Before long he's on the phone, ordering a hamburger and french fries and an ice tea. "What do you want, Sarah?"

I'm not hungry. I'm aching and stiff and a bit sad. "Oh, I don't know. Do they have tuna sandwiches?"

"One tuna sandwich coming up." He conveys the information to the person on the other end of the phone, then hangs up. "Ten minutes, they say."

"That's fast! So, can you untie me now?"

"No, I don't think that I want to do that just yet. I'd like the room service waiter to have the chance to appreciate you."

"No! Please, no." The thought is as horrifying as it is arousing.

"Are you refusing me, Sarah? After all these years, are you going to disappoint me?"

No, not that. I've disappointed him so many times. Broken so many promises, as we both know. This time, today, I want more than anything to please him.

"No—it's okay. If that's what you want."

He sits down next to me, gently brushes my hair away from my face. "Good girl. You're mine, aren't you, Sarah? Mine to use as I please?"

The old thrill races through my trussed up body. This is what I crave, to be owned, to be cherished. "Yes," I say, so soft that he has to lean close to hear. "I'm yours." And at that moment, as he kisses me, I believe what I am saying with all my heart.

The doorbell shocks us both. "Hush, be still now," he says as he gets up. "Just a moment," he calls to the waiter. He raises the corner of the bedspread and flips it over me, hiding my bound form. Then he goes to the door.

The waiter looks barely twenty, rangy with tousled blond hair. He can't help staring at the strange, shrouded lump that is my body as Eric signs the check. "Is your wife all right?" he asks.

"My wife couldn't be better," Eric replies. I hear an edge in his voice that the waiter probably misses. "We're just playing a little game."

"Hide and seek?"

Eric tries hard not to laugh. "Not exactly...There you go. Thank you."

"Sure thing. Have a nice lunch."

"Oh, we will."

I'm laughing too, in relief and in joy at being alone again. I should have known that he wouldn't risk exposing me that way. Then I think of some of our past encounters, and I'm not so sure.

"I'm always torn," says Eric as he works at undoing my bonds. "Between showing the world what a delicious slut you are, and keeping you all to myself."

I stretch out my legs and groan at the stiffness.

"Sorry to keep you tied up so long. Maybe I got a bit carried away."

"I'm out of shape. Not used to this stuff anymore."

"I'll get you whipped into shape in no time." He hands me my sandwich with a grin. "Here. You've got to keep your strength up.

"You know, it was so hard to decide what to take with me this time. I thought about bringing my laptop and some recent videos. We could watch them together—there's nobody I can really share that sort of kinky stuff with except you. But then I thought we wouldn't have the time...One idea I had was to make a ginger fig for you—you know, a little present after not seeing you for so long. I'd love to see how you react to a spicy plug of raw ginger up your ass. But then I realized that it would dry out on the trip, wouldn't be effective..."

He talks on between bites of his hamburger. I'm content

just to sit here in his presence, my sex still humming from my orgasms, listening to my master, face-to-face with him at last.

After a while, though, both his food and his conversation run out, and we're there, looking at each other, wondering what comes next.

"I want to see you naked," I say finally.

"Well, I want to try out that wooden ruler." So he does, and of course, I like it. I've always been willing to let him experiment on my body. It turns me on like nothing else, to put myself in his hands, to let him investigate the effects of various implements, positions and techniques. Sometimes the sensations are pleasurable. Even if they're not, giving myself to him sends me flying. When we're apart I miss his voice, his hands, his humor, his intelligence, but most of all I miss the roller-coaster thrill of his taking control and his outrageous sexual imagination.

By midafternoon my buttocks are crisscrossed with scarlet streaks and I've shaken through two more climaxes. He seems pleased with himself. Still, he must be frustrated. Certainly there has been a bulge in his trousers ever since my first spanking.

We're stretched out together on the bed. I've taken off the corset. He's still fully clothed. Tentatively, I reach out and stroke his erection. "Aren't you uncomfortable? Don't you want to come?"

"I'm putting it off as long as I can. When I come once, that's usually it for quite a while."

I remember in the early days of our relationship, how he'd jack off all over my bound body and be ready to fuck me twenty minutes later. He reads my thoughts.

"Yeah, well, I was a lot younger then. So were you."

"Eric...what can I do for you?"

He sighs. "You're here. You let me touch you, bind you, beat you. You come for me."

"Is that really enough?"

"Maybe it has to be enough."

"No—you deserve more, Eric."

The bitterness in his laugh wounds me. "I don't even have the right to that much. But if you insist, Sarah, you can suck me." He is already unbuckling his pants.

"Oh, yes!" I'm jubilant, eager to give him even a fraction of the pleasure he has evoked in me. I understand that my submission satisfies him in ways that are deeper than a physical orgasm. But I want him to enjoy the physical side as well.

He sits up in the bed, propped against the headboard. I kneel between his spread thighs. His cock is pale with pulsing purple veins. The skin is stretched so tight, I'm sure that he'll burst the instant that I take him into my mouth.

I'm a bit reticent. None of our previous reunions has included anything like this. I begin by licking him gently, flicking the tip of my tongue across his slit, massaging the bulb, soaking him with my saliva. He tastes salty and a bit sour, unfamiliar. The strangeness makes me see and wonder at how comfortable we are together, generally, despite our long separations.

Soon I am sucking hard, taking his full length down my throat. He's mostly passive, letting me do the work. Only his cock, jumping or twitching in response to my tongue, tells me how he's feeling. Aside from an occasional grunt or moan, he's quiet. Mostly, there's just the squelch of my wet mouth on his smooth flesh.

I want him to come—to thrust, to yell, to flood my mouth with his bitter spunk. I suck on and on, my jaw beginning to ache, feeling terribly inadequate that I can't give my master one good orgasm after he's made me come so many times. I reach out to him with my thoughts, begging him to relax, to trust me, to give himself to me.

And all at once, as if in answer, he quickens. He starts to jerk his cock back and forth between my lips. He arches his back, slamming his rod against my palate, using all the strength of his massive body to stimulate himself. I'm gagging, almost choking, but I don't care. He's finally close. I can feel the fluid pumping up the length of him, pulsing, swelling, and I hold my breath, praying for his release.

When he howls, when his come fills my mouth and flows down my chin, I give thanks for his benediction.

We doze for a while in each other's arms. It has been so long, too long. I often dream of him, of us together, of a time like this. Comfort and peace in the wake of passion, complementary desires satisfied. Two sexual outlaws, offering sanctuary to one another.

The rays of the sun slant in, gilding the wingback chair. It's nearly evening. Soon we'll need to rise. We'll shower together, then I'll put on the bra and panties that I brought, to make myself outwardly respectable. He'll come with me to the station, kiss me tenderly good-bye, and put me on the bus for the two-hour voyage back to my home and my husband. I'll spend those hours feeling my master's marks, reliving these few magic hours.

My master will stay in this room tonight. After all, it's already paid for. It will still smell of my cunt and his come.

My husband will greet my bus. He'll kiss me. He won't ask questions. I'll have dinner with him, feeling guilty and awkward, but grateful for his unselfish acceptance of something he doesn't understand.

Later, there will be poems and postmortems. My master and I will discuss, via email, all the things we didn't do. The alligator clips. The unopened package of condoms.

And we'll dream of the next time outside time, our next reunion.

HUMP DAY

Rachel Kramer Bussel

et's make Wednesday the day—it is called Hump Day, after
all," Corey had said to me with raised eyebrows, the brown
stubble along his chin making me want to reach out and touch it,
as it always did. Lately, though, when I touched him anywhere,
it was more like a sweet caress, a fond embrace, rather than the
rip-each-other's-clothes-off abandon we'd started out with. We
still did it, but with nowhere near the frequency and intensity
we'd once had.

I missed that kind of sex, the kind that came before the daily
duties of marriage turned us into people more likely to curl up
with books or late-night TV than each other. I laughed, but then
he grabbed me and pulled me close, his hands cupping my ass
under my short dress, and I stopped laughing. My husband has
a way of saying things that seem funny one moment, and then
make me ache the next. It was a glimpse of the old Corey, the
always-horny Corey, the one who could set me off with just a
word or a look. We were looking for a way to bring back that

magic, save our marriage from sinking into the abyss of relationships where sex became yet another chore. Sure, we were
scheduling sex, but outside the home, in the only way we could
conceive of to get ourselves out of our rut.

So it came to be that every Wednesday at lunchtime we would
sneak off from our big-time corporate executive jobs—he works
for a best-selling beverage company and I work for a bank where
you probably store your money—and go to a seedy hotel about
twenty blocks south of our midtown offices. Seedy, meaning that
we actually paid by the hour—a fraction of what either of us
make in an hour.

That's part of the charm. There, we're not Corey and Donna,
those twin examples of shining corporate promise. We're not
anyone the people in our circle would know or recognize. We're
not people who could afford a fancier hotel. I don't know
exactly what our alter egos do for a living, but we probably
work the late shift. I take off my makeup when I go, change into
baggy jeans, white sneakers, and a nondescript shirt, leaving my
designer suit and pumps in my car or in my office, adding a coat
over my ensemble, and Corey changes out of his suit. Sometimes
he dresses up special for me, though—he's a cop, or a solider,
someone as far removed from his real self as possible. Once, I
didn't even recognize him. For that single hour, once a week,
we're anyone we want to be.

We deliberately chose a place that rents by the hour, where
lunchtime hookups aren't just common, they're expected. There
are no knowing winks or double entendres; afternoon fucking
is just par for the course for the men who run this hotel, and
this suits us just fine. Ever since we established the routine, we
don't speak of it outside the confines of the hotel unless there's
an emergency. Too much discussion spoils the soup that is our
weekly coupling. I'm kind of a lazy fucker, and I let Corey plan

things for the most part, so I don't really know what to expect when I walk in that room. Sometimes he's there waiting for me, naked, ready to lunge. He may greet me at the door with a hard dick and the only way I'll get inside is to get down on my knees and suck it. Other times, he's got a bottle of massage lotion and insists that I lie down on my stomach, while he spends the excruciatingly long hour working me into a lather, only to send me off without getting to come. Sometimes he tugs me into the shower and fucks me roughly against the wall, hot water beating down on us. Sometimes I'm the maid, and he actually makes me clean the room in nothing but a thong!

I like not knowing what to expect. I like knowing that when I cry out, because he almost always makes me scream in pleasure, someone else, some other stranger, perhaps on her way to get fucked herself, will hear me. Now Wednesday is my lucky day, one of those days where I wake up simply wanting to spend the day getting fucked. We do it other times, too, but on Wednesday mornings, there's a particular hum in the air as we race around getting ready for our jobs. My pussy tingles, my nipples harden as I figure out what to wear under my clothes. I love fancy lingerie, but Taylor, my lunchtime-fucking alter ego, not only can't afford it, but likes to have her clothes ripped off. She shops on St. Mark's for trashy fishnets, wildly colored bras and panties, slutty heels, and fuck-me boots. She has her own little section in my closet. I don't know where Corey keeps his stuff, but there's plenty of stuff, that's for sure.

Today, he wasn't there when I arrived. (We each get our own key.) I wasn't sure what to do. Watch TV? Check my cell phone? Get naked? We only have an hour, that's part of the charm—if we had all day it might get boring. The time clock makes things all the more exciting—nobody misses us for this hour, my secretary knows I can't be reached, though she doesn't know where I go, and has never asked. Let her guess. I thought briefly of what my coworkers would think if they knew I snuck off to fuck my husband each week in a hotel they'd probably be scared of even entering for its potential grime. I thought of what Corey's high-powered bosses would think if they knew what he gets up to here with me each week, what we both allow ourselves to do in the name of anonymity.

Corey made me wait awhile. I eventually stopped looking at my watch, the ticking minutes making me all the more uncertain. It *was* Wednesday, wasn't it? I stepped out of the jeans and plain gray shirt, and the horrid sneakers, to reveal hot pink toes peeking out. I'd kept my socks on in the house last night, wanting to save my pedicure for our special encounter. I, as Taylor, had on a ruffled black thong that kept tugging at the crack between my asscheeks, not to mention my pussy. I stick to silk and cotton bikinis and hipsters myself, but Taylor likes her thongs. The bra is new, too, from a sex shop I ventured into after work one day, when I'd put my Taylor clothes back on and entered a XXX paradise. I'd trembled with desire as I peered at the offerings. I'd browsed the walls—the only other stores I'd entered had been those pretty, clean, well-lighted places, where everyone's smiley and friendly. That's what I prefer, but Taylor likes the seediness, the men not-so-subtly checking her out; she likes to do things that would shock her parents—or her kids. Corey and I haven't taken that plunge yet, but Taylor's a working mom. Her daughter's at school when she gets it on.

I blushed as I browsed the aisles, knowing that I'd be taking whatever I brought home to my house in Westchester, to be tucked away until the next Hump Day, our own little holiday, celebrated every week. So that's how I came to be standing in a ruffled black thong in the stark white room with its spare double bed, lone bedside lamp, and dusty TV. I got under the covers, pulling the thin, scratchy sheet over my body, willing myself to be Taylor. What would she do in such a situation? She has a higher libido than I do, and always carries a Pocket Rocket minivibrator with her. I took it out, wondering what I'd do if Corey deprived me of our weekly hookup. He'd have to have a good excuse. But I willed that possibility from my mind and got onto my stomach, slipping the small toy past my thong.

I turned it on to its lowest setting, letting it buzz against my clit just to get warmed up. I didn't want to come by myself. That's when Corey burst in. The door opened in a flash, then slammed shut. I turned around, and he looked pissed. I was scared for a second. He could hear the vibrator buzzing in the room, so I turned it off. "Goddamnit, Taylor! What do you think you're doing?" he yelled.

I didn't know what answer he was looking for. My heart pounded with both nerves and excitement. Sometimes Corey likes to act like he's angry, spanking out his aggression, screaming at me, and the transition takes a little while to process. I stared back at him like a deer frozen in headlights. "You're supposed to be working, young lady. And here are you are, diddling your-self!" He sounded so horrified, I had to quell my giggles. Corey uncovered my naked body in one quick motion, the sheet thrown to the ground while I lay there, exposed. The toy was off, but it was clear what I'd been doing. "Turn over," he barked.

A swarm of excitement raced through me. For whatever reason, it was never like this at home, surrounded by our clothes, furniture, calendars, clocks, to-do lists. I love our home, how we've built it up into something treasured, ours, but for those very reasons, it can be hard to totally let go. Our home is where we're trying to conceive a child, where we've nursed our sick dog, where we've fought and cried in addition to making love. But here, even if we wind up visiting this particular hotel room again, it's not our room. It belongs to an endless stream of people who use it for their own purposes, and because I know we are just borrowing it, I can offer myself to Corey the way I do.

I flipped over so my ass was there for the taking. "Turn the toy back on if it means that much to you," he said. So I did, slipping the vibe beneath me and letting it hum against my clit, and that's when I heard and felt the first smack. "Pick a number, Taylor," he said, slamming into me again. My bottom started to blush as he picked up both speed and intensity.

I offered my age. "Twenty-eight."

He just kept going, as if he hadn't heard me. "Next time, I'm going to bring a friend, so you can suck my cock while he spanks you. What do you think about that, Taylor?" I didn't care who I was anymore, as long as I could experience the wonderful sensations that Corey—or whoever he was today—and the toy were producing in me.

"Now count for me, before I send you back to work. I see cobwebs in the corner of the room." His hand came down extra hard, and I squeaked out "One," and almost before I was done, the next blow was landing. He held each cheek taut before he delivered the smacks, making them hurt even more, but hurt in the way I liked, the way I wanted, the way that made me melt into a puddle of liquid, disappearing into the thin sheets, collapsing against the old, creaky bed.

I made it up to my age, and we both knew I could take more, but Corey immediately pulled me around so I could suck his cock. "You can keep the toy on, but only if you do a good job," he said. I nodded, and then the round head of his circumcised dick was against my lips. I opened and he shoved me down onto him. "Suck it, you whore," he said, and I shivered as he said the magic word. He could never, would never, call me that at home, but here it seemed fitting. I closed my eyes and let him ease me up and down his length, fine-tuning the blow job to his specifications. I love sucking his dick, love feeing him harden against my tongue, love knowing just how much pleasure I can give him. But this was about control; he wasn't gonna tell me how good it felt or give me any praise at all. In fact, he pulled his dick out at one point and slapped it against my cheek, then pinched me there. My pussy responded, frantically moving, clenching against itself, hoping this meant that soon it would get filled with his cock.

I'd have to make do with my fingers and the vibe, because Corey was intent on coming in my mouth. I tried to tune out my pussy's needs and really be his whore, be his to do with as he pleased. "Suck it good, Taylor," he said, his voice extra loud, and I knew he was hoping someone in another room or out in the hall would overhear. He'd probably have gladly let a stranger in to watch. "No more vibrator, Taylor," he said, lifting me off his cock and reaching down to take it away from me. "Maybe later."

He was being mean now, just to show that he was in control. I could've hated him for it, if it didn't make me so wet. Me, Taylor, whoever; my pussy was dripping, literally, wetness rolling down my thighs, making me slick there as I once again deep-throated him, this time kneeling on the ground while he sat with his legs apart, hands roaming over my head, my hair, my shoulders, my back. When they sank into the back of my neck, that always tender, always sensitive spot, my throat truly opened up and I felt the round head of his dick that I love so much hit the back of my throat. "Yeah, yeah, right there," he said, holding me tight as he humped upward into me. Hump. Hump. Hump. And then he came, granting me more than a mouthful of his salty cream, which I did my best to swallow, though some dripped out. I returned to lick up what I'd missed before he mashed my lips to his.

I sank back against the wall, my eyes closed, my body spent in a new kind of way. My nipples were hard, my pussy still on alert, when Corey pressed something into my hand. I opened my eyes to see a red fluffy duster, its feathers bright and bold in the otherwise drab room. "Like I said, there are cobwebs. You better get started." I just gave him a wry smile and started to clean, yet when I bent over to get at the imaginary cobwebs, fingers were thrust into my cunt. Two, then three, then four, until I banged the wall with my fist before letting out a cry of joy and release. I banged the wall again, then heard a corresponding bang from the other side. Oh, wow—someone *was* listening to us. "Better hurry, Taylor. Your shift's over in ten minutes." We made the most of our remaining time. He left before me, and when I rushed out, my cheeks matched the color of the duster tucked into my bag, and I was counting the minutes until the next Hump Day.

GUILTY PLEASURE

Elizabeth Coldwell

They have given me one of the best suites in the hotel. The bed is large enough for three people to sleep together in comfort, the bathroom contains a whirlpool tub and a complimentary selection of expensive lotions and potions, and the huge, triple-glazed window looks out across the panoramic spread of the city, nineteen stories below. It is a suite designed for lovers, and in other circumstances, I would be thinking of the spectacular sex that Don and I could have on that bed, in that bath, or up against that window. But Don isn't here with me, and I can't wait to leave.

I have spent the last seven hours locked in a windowless room with my fellow members of the jury, as we tried to reach a verdict in what the media has been calling "the trial of the century." You know the story—the papers and prime-time news broadcasts have been discussing nothing else for weeks now. Soap star Lily Charteris is accused of killing her boytoy lover with a champagne bottle during a blazing row after he told her he was leaving her for another, younger woman. For weeks now, we've sat and listened to the evidence; tried not to be swayed by the woman's celebrity or the charismatic personality of the lawyer defending her. We all said we were determined that justice should be done—but even with the best of intentions, we just found ourselves arguing points of detail and going over the same ground again and again, until we were finally told that we would have to continue our deliberations in the morning. We've been checked into the hotel, and had our cell phones confiscated so we can have no contact with the outside world, no conversations that might prejudice our decisions or give away some juicy detail of the case. I'm pretty sure a couple of the other jurors have already done deals with the tabloid press to sell their stories once the verdict has been delivered, but that's not why I'm missing my mobile. I don't want to speak to anyone about anything relating to the blood-spattered crime scene and Lily Charteris' erratic flight from her home in her lover's car. I just want to hear Don's voice as he talks me through the mundane details of his day, then steer the conversation round to juicier matters.

When I can't be with my husband, nothing turns me on like talking dirty to him over the phone. I love that deep, sexy voice of his telling me to undress for him, demanding that I describe everything I'm feeling as I slide my fingers into my panties to discover how hot and juicy I'm getting. Once he rang me when he was away on business, while I was driving to pick up the groceries and he was lying on his hotel bed, naked and still wet from the shower. He got me so excited, I nearly crashed the car as he told me how he was stroking his cock and wishing I was there to suck it for him.

I need to stop thinking about our calls, because it's just making things worse, leaving me with an itch that I'm growing increasingly desperate to scratch. What I'm going to have to do is make my own entertainment. I'll fill the tub and dump in plenty of that honey- and vanilla-scented bubble bath that is sitting on the marbled bath surround. I'll raid the minibar, pour myself a generous drink and then, when I'm all nice and relaxed, I'll take out my old faithful vibrator, which is lurking in the bottom of my valise, and I'll bring myself to a much-needed orgasm or two.

It's amazing how planning a little "me time" never fails to perk you up. I'm even humming some stupid little tune as I turn on the taps and pour half the bottle of bubble bath into the tub. Once I'm undressed, I pull out my vibrator and one of the little sachets of lube I always carry around with me, and toss them onto the bed for later. All I need to do now is make a sortie into the minibar. It yields a couple of miniatures of London gin and a can of tonic water, but there's no ice. And you can't have a decent G and T without ice. Technically, we're not supposed to leave our rooms, but with no means of calling down to the front desk for assistance, what else can I do? I throw on the white terry-cloth dressing gown that is hanging up in the wardrobe, relishing the softness of the thick, fluffy material against my skin, and pad into the hall, barefoot, to look for the ice machine.

I find it in a little cubbyhole of a room, just round the corner from the elevator. It's alongside a vending machine, and standing in front of that, debating which of the two dozen available candy bars to spend his loose change on, is one of my fellow jury members, Craig. He turns when he hears me coming, and smiles. Now, Craig has a sleepy, sexy smile, and with his floppy, caramel-colored hair and surfer boy build, he's one of the cutest guys I've met in a long while. If I were ten years younger and single, I'd have been seriously flirting with him these past few weeks. As it is, we've often sat together at lunch, and I've gotten to know a little about him. He's a session musician, hoping to get his big break while he lays down backing tracks for more famous singers, and the stories he shares with me about the gigs he's played and the people he's met are far more glamorous than anything I can tell him about my life as a stay-at-home house-wife. Sometimes, when we talk, it feels like he's holding eye contact a fraction longer than someone who's just being friendly, but that's probably just my imagination.

The candy bar he's chosen is pushed out by the machine to land with a solid thud in the tray at the bottom. Craig sticks a manicured hand in and fishes it out. "I know it's no good for my waistline, but—" he says with a grin, as though he has to worry about what he eats. There's not a stray ounce of fat on him; I should know, I've studied that body of his enough times. "You've got to do something to pass the time."

"Don't worry about it," I reply, as I fill the bucket I've brought from my room with ice. "I'm turning to drink."

"That sounds like a great idea," he says. He looks me up and down slowly, and I'm pretty sure he's realized I'm naked under the robe. "It'd be nice if I could join you."

We've been told that we're not supposed to mix with the other jurors before tomorrow, but I've already broken the rules by coming out here to the hall. And as Craig and I are both of a mind regarding the verdict anyway, there's little danger of one of us influencing the other to change our opinion. At least, that's what I tell myself as I blurt out, "Why don't you? To be honest, I could use some company."

Within moments we're back at my room, and I'm fumbling with the card key.

"Nice room," Craig says, looking around. "And that view is superb. All I can see out of my window is the parking lot."

He turns out to be a vodka man, and I'm unscrewing a bottle

and pouring it into a glass for him when he suddenly says, "Hey, I'm not interrupting anything here, am I?"

The bathroom door is open, and at first I assume he can see the tub, full of foamy water. And then I realize he's staring at the bed—more specifically, at the hot pink vibrator that is still lying where I threw it.

My cheeks are flushed and I know I've been busted. "What can I say?" I ask, trying to make a joke out of the situation. "Sometimes I just get horny."

"Particularly when hubby and his big, hard cock aren't around to satisfy you, huh?" Hearing Craig use the word *cock* makes my pussy clench with a sudden, fierce spasm. As I stand rooted to the spot, he picks the toy up, twists the base so it buzzes briefly into life, then switches it off again. "You know," he says, "I've always wanted to watch a woman use one of these things on herself." I think I know what's coming next, but I just fiddle with my glass as he continues, "And I'd love it if that woman was you."

I should stop the conversation here and ask him to leave the room. After all, I'm a respectable married woman, not some kind of slut who'll act out any old nasty fantasy if a man asks her to. And yet, there's something about being in this anonymous hotel room, away from everyone and everything I know, which makes me feel that, if only for tonight, I could be that slut.

The tension in the room is almost unbearable as Craig takes a swig of his vodka and I wait for him to raise the stakes. "Go on," he says finally. "Take that robe off for me."

I set down my glass and walk over to the bed. Craig's eyes never leave me as my hands fumble with the belt of the robe. I untie it and shrug the garment off, standing before him naked. It's been a very long time since anyone but Don has seen me this way, and I can't help being a little insecure as I bare myself to him. I'm sure my body is more mature than those of the girls

Craig is used to being with, a little heavier, a little more rounded. But his gaze is eating me up, letting me know just how desirable he finds me.

"Here." Craig hands me the vibrator, letting his hand brush gently against the curve of my ass. I don't bother with the lube; I'm already so wet that I know the toy is just going to slip inside me.

"How do you want me?" I ask.

"It's up to you," he says. "You're running the show."

So I settle myself in the chair by the bed, and hook one leg over the arm, spreading myself wide. It's a position that gives him a perfect view of my neatly waxed sex, its petals already peeling apart to show him the pink secrets inside. As I switch on the vibrator, I can't help but notice that Craig's pants seem noticeably tighter around the crotch. It seems like my wanton display is having an effect already.

As Craig watches, I run the toy along the insides of my thighs, warming myself up for what's to come. Usually, I like to run some kind of fantasy in my head to help build my excitement, but what's happening here makes all that unnecessary. I caress my breasts, losing myself in my own pleasure. Then, as my need becomes more urgent, I slide the vibrator gently up and down my slit, feeling the sensations all the way to my core. The buzzing of the toy and the soft hum of the air-conditioning are the only sounds in the room, and I close my eyes, almost forgetting I have an audience as I press the cool plastic just a little way into my hole.

"Hey, that's enough," I hear Craig say. "I don't want you coming." I'm just about to remind him that I'm supposed to be the one in charge here, and then he adds, "Well, not without my cock inside you."

This is a line I didn't expect to cross. Playing with myself in front of another man doesn't count as cheating—at least, that's how I've rationalized what I've done so far—but letting him fuck me? And as he unzips his pants and brings out his cock, long and smooth and hard, I can't deny that I want him to. The nice wife I usually am would object, but not the slut I've become for the night. This is nothing more than a guilty pleasure, I tell myself, as I let Craig haul me from the chair and push me so I'm bending over the bed, with him behind me. It's just a one-time thing that doesn't change the way I feel about the husband I love.

Craig doesn't even bother to undress, he's so desperate to have me, and as I turn my head, I catch a glimpse of the two of us reflected in the mirror of the vanity. There's something so dirty about the sight of him, his cock jutting from his zip as he lines it up with the entrance to my cunt. He pushes his way inside me and I groan, gripping handfuls of the bedcovers. Toys may have their uses, but they can't compare to the feel of a hot, solid cock filling you up.

He grabs me by the hips and begins to pump, pulling me back onto him with every thrust. He doesn't know my body the way Don does, doesn't know just where to touch me or the way I like to be fucked, but his hard, young body and his enthusiasm make up for all of that. We're both moaning and yelling, making so much noise that for a moment I worry they'll be able to hear us in the next room—and then I stop worrying about everything as Craig presses the vibrator to my clit and my orgasm rushes unstoppably through me.

Craig holds me in his arms, my flushed and sweating body pressing against his T-shirt-clad chest, and he tells me how wonderful I am, and how lucky my husband is to have me.

Tomorrow, he says, this trial will be over and we'll both go back to our own lives, but he'll never forget what happened tonight and how good it was. And as he leaves to go back to his own room, I know I don't have to feel guilty about anything.

AN HONEST WOMAN

Tenille Brown

In her days as an honest woman, Ruth never would have even considered this. If someone had even so much as whispered the idea to her, she would have simply frowned and turned up her nose.

But, Ruth was no longer an honest woman, which was why she sat on a double bed in a corner room of the Bluebird Inn wringing her hands as she waited for a man named Marvin to come fuck her.

It was just that simple. Ruth giggled at the thought. She giggled because all things considered, she and Marvin *were* going to fuck.

And the best part was that no one knew. Not her sister or her daughter, not even her bingo buddies.

Hell, Ruth was a grown woman and the last time she checked, it was a free country. She wasn't anybody's wife, not anymore, and most of all, Ruth was fifty years old, and she was beyond being coy.

And it wasn't like Ruth *couldn't* do it in her own house. But doing it there added pressure. There was the expected hospitality, like meals prepared in her kitchen, conversations in her den. It could complicate things and this thing she and Marvin had, it wasn't complicated, never had been, and she intended to keep it that way.

Ruth checked her watch again even though she knew Marvin wouldn't be late. It was the way of the truckers; they got there on time.

He had called last week to talk specifics. It was one of the few times he ever used her phone number, and it was the only time Ruth waited for the phone to ring. It was the only time she got antsy and impatient, like her inner alarm knew when to start ticking relentlessly.

Ruth had met Marvin at a diner eight years ago. Her husband Sal had been gone two years by then, and Ruth had taken to going to local flea markets on Saturday to kill time. During a busy lunch hour one day, she had accepted a cup of coffee and a slice of pie from a stout, dark brown man with a beard and took him up on an offer to accompany him to his motel room across the way.

Back then, he disguised his desire for her with the request of her company while he fell asleep, but when they lay down beside each other in the double bed, it was clear that sleep was the farthest thing from either of their minds.

She remembered how she had sat there on the bed in this very same motel like it was as familiar to her as her own skin, like she had seen the insides of motel rooms many times over when really she had only stayed in one once and that was with Sal on their wedding night.

Now it was routine, like a physical. This thought made Ruth giggle again.

Once a year, Marvin passed through. Once a year, Ruth packed a satchel, told her neighbor she was going to visit her grandbabies and drove fifty miles out where the vacancy sign flashed neon orange and a room was already reserved, and the desk clerks knew her by the name Rosa.

It was room 313 this time; she had left it on his voice mail. It was a modest room, this one, small, clean. She had never desired more than that. She didn't need room service or a bar downstairs. She didn't need a bellhop or an indoor pool.

All she needed was already here, a bed she didn't have to make in a room she didn't have to clean, and soon she would be fucking the good sense out of a ruggedly handsome man who wouldn't ask her to make a sandwich after.

The sound of Marvin's rig pulling into the truck stop next door shook Ruth from her thoughts. In the idle moments between the slamming of the truck door and his footsteps on the walkway, she knew he was picking up a Coke and a bag of chips for himself, some nabs and a Pepsi for her.

Minutes later, there were three soft knocks. Ruth stood up, smoothed her hair, straightened her pants, and opened the door.

Marvin wore a plaid shirt tucked into his cargo jeans, dusty work boots, and a cap pulled way down on his head. The past year had been good to him, only adding about seven or eight pounds to his midsection and a little extra gray throughout his short, coarse hair. His shoulders were still broad and strong, his smile white, and his hands...

Ruth's eyes drifted down to those magical tools he used to rub, tickle, and finger her, but today they held something foreign, something that made Ruth step back and clear her throat.

"What's that?" She pointed.

Ruth asked the question before she even said hello, before she could begin pretending to care how he had been getting along the past several months.

Marvin chuckled and stepped inside, brushing gently past her.

"Well, hello to you, too, Ruth," he said and leaned over to peck her lightly on the cheek. "And this happens to be a rose. Might be silly, I know, but I saw it over there at the truck stop and, well, I know you never mentioned either way your feelings on flowers, so I figured I'd try you out."

Ruth shrugged and took the long-stemmed yellow object from his hand. "Oh, I like flowers just fine. Planted some lilies just a few weeks ago as a matter of fact."

Marvin seemed satisfied with that response. He handed her the bag of snacks next, then placed his overnight case on the floor beside the dresser.

Marvin rubbed the front of his jeans, his eyes darting about the room.

He was nervous. Eight years, same motel, fucking in the parking lot, the small outside pool, and on the floor, and he had the gumption to be nervous.

"Lilies, eh?" Marvin asked. "I bet they're pretty. Maybe you could show 'em to me sometime—"

And that was when Ruth decided to kiss him, soft and slow, get this party started once and for all. Maybe that was what happened to men in their old age, they got fidgety and soft and emotional like...like a woman. Ruth took Marvin's hands and placed them on her hips.

It silenced Marvin, if nothing else, and she felt his body begin to relax. He brought his hands up to her middle and pulled her to him. He nuzzled her neck, planting gentle kisses on her nutmeg skin.

And Ruth was thankful that he finally gave in to the silence because frankly, she didn't care much for the talking, she never had. She hadn't been obligated to carry on small talk since Sal died, and now all she cared to know was that Marvin still moved like liquid, that he was still generous and adventurous with his tongue, and that he could still touch her and make her skin tingle.

Marvin proved to still be able to do all those things and they undressed quickly, stepping out of their clothes with the enthusiasm of hungry animals that were waiting to be fed.

Marvin stepped back, admiring Ruth's mature bareness and Ruth allowed this for a bit, until she decided she wanted to enjoy a certain view herself.

She took him in her hands.

Mercifully, Marvin was already hard.

His excitement swelled and bounced between his thick thighs. Ruth continued to stroke him slowly and steadily as her own desire peaked. Moisture kissed the insides of her thighs. Her nipples hardened and her skin grew warm and it was then that she let Marvin guide her to the bed.

They didn't bother to pull back the covers. They didn't close the drapes. They didn't care that they kicked the phone off the nightstand and knocked all the pillows off the bed.

Marvin turned Ruth around and positioned himself behind her. He guided his solid penis inside of her. She pulled at the covers, holding them against her breasts. Sweat ran down her body and onto the sheets and she didn't care. After all, she wouldn't have to wash them.

Ruth moved in front of Marvin in smooth, fluid movements. The feel of him inside her sent waves of pleasure coursing through her body. Heat started inside her and floated out.

Cars passed furiously on the highway. Strangers in the next room frantically bumped the headboard against the wall. Water in a room up top dripped in the bathroom sink.

And in this room, number 313, the bed creaked.

Marvin groaned and held tighter to Ruth's healthy hips.

He grunted. Ruth smiled, knowing he would come soon and it would be okay to release her own climax. Marvin's body stiffened with his orgasm and he pushed her slightly forward. Ruth's nipples pressed gently against the firm mattress.

Then, Ruth screamed and silence once again filled the room.

Ruth had been listening to Marvin's soft snores for over an hour. She reached for her Pepsi, her nabs, and the remote control.

She looked over at Marvin, so peaceful, so content. She wondered if he had been the same way with his former wife, before he had begun traveling, seeing the world, meeting people and doing things.

Marvin had married young—he had revealed this in earlier conversations—and it was around that time that he discovered his love of the road. Soon he began to stay gone more than he was home, and he popped up at his house one afternoon only to find out that his young wife was keeping time with their tax man.

It was after that, Marvin said, that he stayed away from women, that his rig was his woman, but then he saw Ruth, smelled how sweet she was, and figured even an old dog could change his ways every now and then.

And Ruth decided she appreciated this about him, and now, at a quarter 'til eleven, she would appreciate it once more. Ruth started to rouse Marvin, her hands between his legs, rubbing his cock to rigid awakening.

She straddled him and guided him inside of her. Ruth rode Marvin until they both shivered and settled, content, beneath the crisp white sheets.

* * *

Ruth awakened to the sharp smell of ham and eggs. When she opened her eyes, Marvin was sitting at the table in a corner of the room, a goofy grin plastered on his face.

"I thought you might be hungry, so I got you a little something from the diner."

Ruth nodded. She rubbed her eyes and sat up in bed. The covers fell down into her lap and she quickly retrieved them, shielding her nudity.

"You didn't have to go through the trouble," she said. "I'm not really a breakfast person."

Marvin shook his head. "Oh, it was no trouble. I get up early, anyway, and you were pretty far gone and I hated to disturb you, so I went over and had some breakfast. I brought this back for you just in case."

Suddenly, Ruth was no longer concerned about her nakedness. She walked over and rubbed Marvin's back. "On second thought, I am a little hungry. But ham and eggs weren't really what I had a craving for." She reached down and toyed with his belt.

Marvin placed his hand over hers, stopping her.

"Ruth, I went over to that diner to think some things over."

Ruth's hands dropped at her sides.

"Oh," she said. "Well?"

"Well," Marvin said, "I was thinking I might be done with all this. I'm thinking about parking my rig and putting down roots somewhere."

There, he had said it.

And Ruth said, "Look, Marvin, if this is your way of letting me down easy, then you don't even have to waste your time. I'm a grown woman and you don't have to waste your games on me."

Ruth thought she sounded more disappointed than she intended, so she folded her lips and locked her hands behind her back.

Now irritated, Ruth narrowed her eyes and cocked her head. She knew good-bye when she saw it. She turned around, gathering her things to go, fighting to keep the expression on her face as neutral as she could. It had come unexpectedly, yes, but Ruth had known that it would end sometime.

Marvin shook his head. "No, Ruth, that's not it at all. I was just trying to find a way to tell you that, well…"

Marvin grabbed Ruth by the wrist. And without looking at her, he began to speak. "I want you to know that I don't see anybody besides you."

Ruth nodded, listening, unsure of exactly where he was going with this.

"And, Ruth," he continued, "I don't care to see anybody but you."

"Just what exactly are you saying, Marvin?" She turned and looked at him.

Marvin exhaled and closed his eyes. He rubbed his palms on his thighs, then opened his eyes again.

"I'm saying, Ruth, that I'd like to marry you, if you don't mind—make an honest woman out of you."

Ruth tilted her head. "I've been an honest woman, Marvin. Was one for twenty years."

Marvin nodded. "And I get that, I do. But here we are doing this thing for all these years, and I'd like to think we've built at least a little something between us. I mean, don't you need things, like your yard taken care of or someone to take you to town when you need it?"

Ruth shrugged. "Joe's been doing my yard for years. I have a plumber and a mechanic and—"

"And someone to meet at the Bluebird Inn who'll tighten you up once a year."

Ruth's lips snapped shut.

She wished Marvin would just tell the damned truth. That he was getting older, moving slower. That his joints ached and his eyes weren't what they used to be. That he couldn't handle the rig anymore and it was time for him to hang up his hat.

A moment of awkward silence passed between them.

"Well," Marvin said, splitting the silence clear down the middle. "I suppose I did spring this on you all at once, me and my crazy ideas. Tell you what, you think on it awhile. I'm gonna grab a shower."

Ruth watched Marvin walk toward the bathroom, unbuttoning his shirt to reveal a white undershirt that clung to his solid chest.

Then it came to Ruth just what would get Marvin's mind off it all, what could push all this marriage foolishness right out of his idiotic head.

She waited to hear the sound of the shower. She crept into the bathroom naked and joined Marvin behind the pale yellow curtain.

Marvin was startled at her entrance. She felt it when he shivered at her touch as though the water were ice-cold. He relaxed when she stepped up close behind him and slipped her hands around his waist. She massaged his cock to attention.

Marvin turned to face her.

"Ruth, I—"

And then she kissed him. Every time he looked as though he wanted to speak, she slipped her tongue inside his mouth. Every time he got that boyish twinkle in his eyes, she wrapped her hand tighter around his cock and stroked.

Finally, Marvin gave in. He pushed all conversation aside and lifted Ruth's leg. He pressed her back against the shower wall and worked his way inside of her. Marvin fucked Ruth slow and steady as the water came down and the steam billowed around them.

Ruth let the water saturate her hair and run down her shoulders as she marveled at the feel of Marvin between her legs. Her fingers slid down his back.

She came before she was ready, shivering even in the heat of the shower. She forced herself still enough to wait for Marvin, and he followed minutes later, coming inside her with a force that pinned her body against the warm, wet wall.

Ruth watched in silence as Marvin got dressed.

There were things she didn't know about him. Things she didn't want or need to know. Like, if he was a drinker and what kind of music he liked and over the years, if he had taken to popping Viagra or if was he still naturally blessed with the gift of a strong, solid cock.

There were also things he didn't know about her, like how at home, she never, ever slept naked, not even when Sal was alive, that she only cooked when she felt like it, and she didn't clean nearly as much as she should.

Ruth appreciated all those hidden truths, and until now, she thought Marvin did, too.

It was getting close to eleven. Right about now they should have been saying their abbreviated good-byes, smiling politely. Marvin should have been seeing her to her car, Ruth calling once she got home to make sure he had started out on the road okay, and that would be the end of it until next time.

But instead, the loud silence stood between them like a pink elephant.

Ruth supposed she did love Marvin on some level. After all, they *had* been doing this for eight years and for a moment, she thought to tell him so, but it was Marvin who spoke first, his voice low, not even looking at her.

"So, Ruth, what do you say?"

And Ruth shrugged and half-smiled and she said, "Okay."

Marvin's lips quivered. Nervous, he walked from wall to wall rubbing his palms against his cheeks.

"That's real good news, Ruth," he said. "I'm real happy to hear you say that. I've got a couple more loads before I'll get another few days off, but I can come through at the end of next week. What do you say we meet up here then and discuss details?"

Ruth nodded. "Yes, yes, of course, Marvin. That sounds fine."

When the final lie slipped from her lips, Ruth looked at him one last time.

She'd miss Marvin; she knew she would, and it was a damned shame. They could have had something special.

Maybe Ruth was an honest woman after all. She pondered the idea the next week as she parked her car in front of the sparsely populated coffeehouse on the corner. She was thinking of how honest she could be as she sat beside a mustached trucker who winked and offered to pay for her tea and cake.

And honestly, if this handsome gentleman invited her to that little motel around the way for a little talking and TV watching, Ruth was thinking that might be just fine.

ROOM SERVICE

Donna George Storey

Hotel rooms turn me on. The blankness, the anonymity, that big bed begging you to strip off its tacky flowered spread and indulge in sensual excess. It's not just me. I've found things in my travels: European porn with captions in four languages stuffed in a phone book, a single black stocking behind a chair.

Even now that I'm flying east so often for my job, I still get a twinge at that first whiff of Lysol-spiked air. Tonight I'm in Atlanta. The room has an appropriately antebellum décor, the TV and minibar tucked away in a mahogany cabinet, the silhouette of a lady in a hoop skirt in an oval frame above the bed.

I hang up my garment bag and head for the window. I'm eighteen stories up, but the street sounds still reach me through the chilly glass. Toy-sized SUVs and motorcycles speed along Peachtree Road, human shadows hurry under the neon. Your typical city in evening dress, restless with possibility.

I'm restless tonight, too. Maybe it's the splayed legs on the brocade armchair, or the thick wooden knobs on the drawers.

Or maybe it's that my coworker Kevin has the next room, the one right through that door by the closet.

Ah, Kevin. My sales engineer, and the perfect nice guy. He's not bad looking either, with his gold-green eyes and size 32 pants (I checked the label on his jeans). His hands are his best feature, though, thick fingered and tireless. I sat across the aisle from him on the flight out and watched him working on his laptop. The regional sales manager told Kevin just this morning he wanted tomorrow's presentation rewritten so it matches the customer's RFP, and he was none too happy about it. I expressed my sympathy, but secretly I enjoyed his scowl of concentration, the steady tap of his index finger on the touchpad. It reminded me of the way I masturbate.

Kevin's married, of course. I've met his wife. I like her. As far as I'm concerned, his marital status is one of his many attractive qualities. I'm still recovering from a nasty breakup and see no reason to waste my ambivalent, on-the-rebound lust on someone I could actually have.

Without really thinking, I smooth my pin-striped skirt over my belly and let my fingers wander lower to press the rough cloth up between my thighs. With a quick shake of my head, I snatch my hand away and pull the curtain closed. Hardly proper behavior for a newly promoted product manager: playing with herself in front of a hotel window.

The only thing to do now is get ready for bed. Flossing my teeth always puts me back in a wholesome frame of mind. On my way to the bathroom, I resist the urge to try the door to Kevin's room. What if it opened and he were undressing or even jacking off to one of those pay-per-view videos? I've never had the nerve to rent one, especially on a business trip. I've heard the women in accounting laughing over the hotel receipts. They know.

Not that I need a video. It's enough to put on my nightgown and slip under the sheets, breathing in the fragrance of hotel linen. When I close my eyes, I can see them. I smell them, too, beneath the semen-scented tang of bleach, all the people who've sought their pleasure on this bed.

My husband never takes me this way, a woman whispers. In the fading afternoon light, she straddles her lover, hips tucked under, and glides the head of his cock past her pussy to the prim, virgin opening beyond.

A gray-haired man, nude but for an undershirt, sits at the edge of the bed, his eyes fixed on the rouged nipples of the girl from the escort service as she sinks to her knees and takes him between her practiced lips.

I'm part of it now, floating on that river of lust. I turn over on my stomach and rest my forehead on the pillow, my own breath rising hot against my cheeks. I rock my pelvis into the mattress, bending my knees slightly to keep my thighs tense. It's an old college trick that came in handy on nights when I was horny but wasn't sure my roommate was asleep.

I hear a soft knock. The door clicks open.

"Hey, Sara, you still up?"

"Kevin?"

"Don't turn around."

It's not his usual friendly but respectful tone. At first I'm annoyed. He has some nerve ordering me around when I'll be helping to evaluate him for a raise next month.

"By the way, I didn't mean to interrupt you." The voice moves closer. "Keep moving your hips against the bed. I liked that."

I smile into the pillow. "Here I thought you liked me for my interesting mind."

"I do." He laughs. "I wouldn't be here without it. But there's no denying you've got dangerous curves."

My back starts to tingle. Funny how a man can do that to you, just by staring.

"Do you like to be taken from behind?" Kevin asks.

My cunt muscles clench, then flutter.

I see a woman on all fours, trembling as the man behind her guides his ruddy shaft toward her fleshy cunt lips. *You're gonna come this way, you sweet bitch, and I won't stop fucking you until you do.*

It happened right here on this bed.

"I like it," I admit, "but I have to be really hot or I have trouble coming."

"Ah, well, then let's get you warmed up." Kevin's voice is gentle. "Pull down the sheet and lift up your nightgown so I can see you."

I hesitate, suddenly shy. But Kevin and I want the same thing. I kick down the covers and hike the gown up to my waist. The air feels cool on my bare skin.

Kevin grunts his approval. "Nice. Has anyone ever come here? On your back?"

"No. My tits, sure. They all want to do that."

"Typical," he snorts. "Those guys don't know what they're missing. Such satiny skin. And you're all flushed. I'd say you're warm already."

"Yes. But I need more. Would you touch me?"

"It's tempting, but you know I can't do that."

"We don't have to fuck. You can use your fingers. Or lick me. Anything you want."

"Sorry, Sara, I can't. My wife's already hassled me about going on a business trip with a sexy older woman. If she asks any questions, I have to be able to say I never laid a hand on you."

Clever boy to have figured out the angles.

"I've got another idea," he says. "You and Mr. Mattress used to have a pretty good time back in college. You two can get reacquainted while I jerk off on your beautiful ass."

The sudden gush of wetness says my pussy likes the idea. "Can I play with my clit?"

Kevin thinks a moment. "Try it without this time, Sara. Everyone knows you like a challenge."

"I have to touch my nipples." In fact, I am known as a tough negotiator around the office.

"All right," Kevin concedes. "You can play with your tits. But hands off below the waist."

"Agreed. But you have to come first." This is important. When I'm all turned on, I love a man's spunk. I slather it over my chest and paint it on my lips and lick it off drop by drop. But if he comes after I do, I go straight for the Kleenex.

"Maybe, boss." There's a smile in his voice. "But you have to earn it."

"Cheeky bastard," I mutter, though of course his new cockiness is turning me on. But I've got my strategy. I start grinding my hips like I used to at college dances, when I let the bass throb up through me, when I knew guys were watching. Every now and then I add a little shimmy. That shadow fucking used to turn me on, too.

"That's right. Dance for me, baby," Kevin croons. His voice slips inside me, like a teasing finger, but it's not just his voice, it's other sounds, too, a zipper being undone, the rhythmic click of hand stroking cock, ragged breathing intermingled with low groans. He's standing at the edge of the bed now—I can see it—his hard-on poised over the hillocks of my ass like a canon over an old battlefield.

I slide one hand up under my breast and pinch my nipple, twist it. The sheet beneath me is damp with a growing stain of pussy juice and sweat.

"Come on me," I whisper, thrusting my hips harder. The mattress lets out faint squeaks of pleasure.

There's no answer, but I know his hand's moving faster, tiny folds of flesh gathering at the head of his penis with each upward stroke.

"Come on my ass. Now," I say louder.

He must have remembered that evaluation, because suddenly I hear a sharp intake of breath, like he's been punched, then I feel it, I really do, come pelting my hips, dribbling into my cleft like summer rain. Something warm—his hand?—spreads the soapy slickness over my skin, probing my crack, drawing circles and figure-eights over the tender skin. When he finds the sweetest spot he starts to tap—open file, open file—and open I do as electric jolts shoot up my spine. I'm banging against the mattress for all I'm worth and suddenly the hand grows, huge and hot, as it grips the muscles of my cunt, my thighs, my whole fucking body and squeezes, over and over and over again.

When the sweat cools, I pull down my nightgown and roll onto my back, wiggling my fingers at the empty air.

"Look, Ma, no hands."

I'm part of history now, all the couplings of fantasy and flesh this bed has known.

The phone jangles on the nightstand.

"Hey, Sara, you still up?" It's Kevin.

"Yeah, just relaxing," I say. It's not a lie.

"I'm going down to the bar for a beer. Care to join me?"

"Sure. I'll need a few minutes. Meet you there?"

I hang up the phone and smile. I'd gotten his voice just right.

The bar has a *Gone With the Wind* theme, the bartender decked out in a waistcoat, cravat, and close-clipped black mustache,

Rhett Butler style. Some jobs really do ask too much of you.

Kevin's the only customer. He's frowning into his beer, but his face brightens when he sees me.

"Thanks for coming," he says.

"My pleasure. It must feel good to be done with that presentation."

"Oh, I'm not done yet," he says grimly. "I'll do what I can tonight, but after this, McMillan gives me at least a full day's notice on changes or he takes what he's got, customer be damned. I'm gonna set that asshole straight at breakfast tomorrow in no uncertain terms."

I nod, holding back a smile. Kevin's not the confrontational type. That's part of his charm. Still, he's awfully cute when he's mad.

As if he's read my thoughts, he breaks into a sheepish grin. "Listen to me talk. What a fantasy, huh?"

"Oh, I don't know. With the right technique, a little visualization, you might get the result you're looking for."

Kevin gives me a searching look. "Do you really think I can do it?"

I let my fingers brush his hand, a small self-indulgence. His skin is warm, just like I'd imagined.

"Kevin," I say, "you'd be amazed at the things you can do."

ABOUT THE AUTHORS

TENILLE BROWN's writing is featured online and in several print anthologies including *Caught Looking, Ultimate Lesbian Erotica 2007, A Is for Amour, D Is for Dress-Up*, and *The Greenwood Encyclopedia of African American Women Writers*. She obsessively shops for shoes, hats, and purses and keeps a daily blog on her website www.tenillebrown.com.

ELIZABETH COLDWELL is the editor of the UK edition of *Forum*. Her stories have appeared in anthologies including *Sex at the Sports Club, Sex and Shopping, Best Women's Erotica 2006, Spank Me*, and *Yes, Sir*. Her ideal hotel room would indeed come with a whirlpool tub, a big bed, and a cute young man as standard.

ANDREA DALE's stories have appeared in *Hide and Seek, Screaming Orgasms and Sex on the Beach, Naughty or Nice, Got a Minute?*, and *Cowboy Lover*, among others. With coauthors, she has sold novels to Cheek Books (*A Little Night Music,* Sarah Dale, 2007) and Black Lace Books (*Cat Scratch Fever,* Sophie Mouette, 2006). She believes that all hotel rooms should have two beds: one for sleeping and one for sex. Her website is at www.cyvarwydd.com.

TESS DANESI is a writer of erotic fiction with a D/s twist, who also blogs about her varied experiences and often tumultuous life at Urban Gypsy (www.nyc-urban-gypsy.blogspot.com) as well as being a sex toy reviewer for Edenfantasys.com. Tess was a winner of Babeland's erotica contest and has been published in *Time Out New York.*

AMANDA EARL's erotica has been published most recently in *The Mammoth Book of Best Erotica Volume 6 (*Carroll and Graf, 2007), *He's on Top: Erotic Stories of Male Dominance and Female Submission* (Cleis Press, 2007), *Iridescence: Sensuous Shades of Lesbian Erotica* (Alyson Books, 2007), *Cream: The Best of the Erotica Readers and Writers Association* (Thunder's Mouth Press, 2006), in *Front & Centre Magazine,* Volume 18 (Black Bile Press, October, 2007), and on the website Lies with Occasional Truth (www.LWOT.net).

SHANNA GERMAIN's erotic stories have appeared or are scheduled to appear in dozens of publications and anthologies, including *Absinthe Literary Review, Aqua Erotica 2, Best American Erotica, Best Bondage Erotica, Best Gay Romance, Best Lesbian Erotica 2008,* and *The Mammoth Book of Best New Erotica.* She is a fiction editor for Clean Sheets and 42Opus, as well as a poetry editor for the *American Journal of Nursing.* You can see more of her work, erotic and otherwise, on her website, www.shannagermain.com.

ISABELLE GRAY's writing can be found in *First-Timers, Best Date Ever, Iridescence: Sensuous Shades of Lesbian Erotica*, and many others. She, and her other personalities, can be found online at www.pettyfictions.com.

MAXIM JAKUBOWSKI is a writer and ex-publisher who lives in London. He edits and pens erotica, being responsible for *The Mammoth Book of Erotica* series and several novels and short-story collections including *American Casanova, Fools for Lust*, and *Confessions of a Romantic Pornographer*, most recently. In civilian life, he is better known for his crime and mystery books and anthologies and runs London's annual Crime Scene festival, as well as being a regular contributor to the *Guardian* newspaper. He has been known to frequent hotel rooms and has no website. Read into that what you will.

STAN KENT is a chameleon-hair-colored former nightclub owning rocket scientist author of hot words and cool stories. A dedicated voyeur and world traveler, Stan has penned nine original, unique, and very naughty full-length novels including the *Shoe Leather* series and dozens of quickie reads on everything from spanking with shoes to cupcake sex to voyeuristic orgies to techno-rave group spankings on the dance floor. When not globe-trotting and jet-setting, Stan has hosted an erotic talk show night at Hustler Hollywood. The *Los Angeles Times* described his monthly performances as "combination moderator and lion tamer." To see samples of his works, his latest hair colors, and travels, visit Stan at www.StanKent.com or email him at stan@stankent.com.

MADLYN MARCH is the pseudonym of a journalist who has written for the *New York Post*, *Time Out New York*, AfterEllen. com, and many more. She has also been featured in the anthology

First-Timers. Contrary to what you might think, the Jacuzzi people did not pay her any money to write her story.

GWEN MASTERS writes all the time: in her sleep, in the car, even in church. Hundreds of those stories have been published in dozens of places, both in print and online. She hides away in a sleepy Tennessee town, writing naughty novels and rambling about in the century-old home she shares with her journalist husband. For more information on Gwen and her works, visit her website (www.gwenmasters.net) or blog (www.gwenmasters.blogspot.com).

TERESA NOELLE ROBERTS has been known to travel to exotic places and see very little other than the hotel room. Her erotic fiction has appeared in *He's on Top, She's On Top, Caught Looking, Love on the Dark Side, Beyond Desire, Hide and Seek, Best Women's Erotica 2004, 2005,* and *2007, Chocolate Flava 2,* Fishnetmag.com, and many other anthologies, magazines, and websites. She also writes erotica and erotic romance as half of Sophie Mouette. Sophie's novella "Hidden Treasure" appears in Rachel's collection *Bedding Down.*

THOMAS S. ROCHE's short stories have appeared in more than four hundred anthologies, magazines, and websites. He has written, edited, or coedited more than ten books, including the *Noirotica* series of erotic crime-noir stories and the short-story collection *Dark Matter.* He also blogs about sex, drugs, and cryptozoology and occasionally podcasts erotic fiction at www.thomasroche.com.

LISABET SARAI has been writing and publishing erotica since 2000 and has three novels and two short story collections to her credit. She has also edited two erotica anthologies, *Sacred Exchange* and *Cream*. Her stories have appeared in more than a dozen collections including *She's on Top, He's on Top, Cross-dressing, Naughty Spanking Stories from A to Z 1* and *2*, and the past three years' *Mammoth Book of Best New Erotica*. Recently she began ePublishing with Total-E-Bound (www.total-e-bound.com). Lisabet also reviews books and film for the Erotica Readers and Writers Association and Erotica Revealed, and is a Celebrity Author at the Custom Erotica Source. Visit her website at www.lisabetsarai.com.

LILLIAN ANN SLUGOCKI, an award-winning feminist writer, has created a body of work on women and their sexuality which includes fiction, nonfiction, plays, and monologues that have been produced on Broadway, Off-Broadway, Off-Off Broadway, and on National Public Radio. Her work has been published in books, journals, anthologies, and online, including Salon.com. She has been reviewed in the *New York Times*, the *Village Voice, Art in America,* the *New Yorker,* the *New York Daily News,* the *New York Post,* and recently in London, in *Time Out,* the *Guardian,* the *Telegraph,* and the *London Times.*

DONNA GEORGE STOREY's erotic fiction has appeared in more than fifty journals and anthologies including *Dirty Girls; Naughty or Nice; Yes, Sir; He's on Top; She's on Top; Best American Erotica 2006; Mammoth Book of Best New Erotica,* and *Best Women's Erotica.* Her novel, *Amorous Woman,* the intimate story of an American woman's love affair with Japan, was published by Orion in 2007. She currently writes a column "Cooking up a Storey" for the Erotica Readers and Writers Association. Read more of her work at www.DonnaGeorgeStorey.com.

ALISON TYLER is loyal to coffee (black), lipstick (red), and tequila (straight). She has tattoos, but no piercings; a wicked tongue, but a quick smile; and bittersweet memories, but no regrets. She believes it won't rain if she doesn't bring an umbrella, prefers hot and dry to cold and wet, and loves to spout her favorite motto: "You can sleep when you're dead." She chooses Led Zeppelin over the Beatles, the Cure over NIN, and the Stones over everyone—yet although she appreciates good rock, she has a pitiful weakness for '80s hair bands. In all things important, she remains faithful to her partner of more than a decade, but she still can't settle on one perfume. Visit www.alisontyler.com for more luscious revelations or myspace.com/alisontyler, if you'd like to be her friend.

SASKIA WALKER (www.saskiawalker.co.uk) is a British author who has had erotic fiction published on both sides of the pond. You can find her work in many anthologies including *Best Women's Erotica 2006*, *Red Hot Erotica*, *Slave to Love*, *Secrets Volume 15*, *The Mammoth Book of Best New Erotica Volume 5*, *She's on Top*, and *Kink*. Her longer work includes the erotic novels *Along for the Ride* and *Double Dare*.

KRISTINA WRIGHT is an award-winning author who loves writing stories that are emotionally compelling and sexually charged. Her erotic fiction has appeared in more than fifty print anthologies, including *Best Women's Erotica*, *The Mammoth Book of Best New Erotica*, and *Dirty Girls: Erotica for Women*. She holds a BA in English, an MA in humanities, and is completing a certificate in women's studies. For more information about Kristina, visit her website, www.kristinawright.com.

ABOUT
THE EDITOR

RACHEL KRAMER BUSSEL (www.rachelkramerbussel.com) is an author, editor, blogger, and reading series host. She has edited or coedited more than twenty books of erotica, including *Tasting Him; Tasting Her; Spanked: Red-Cheeked Erotica; Naughty Spanking Stories 1* and *2; Yes, Sir; Yes, Ma'am; He's on Top; She's on Top; Caught Looking; Hide and Seek; Crossdressing; Rubber Sex; Sex and Candy; Ultimate Undies; Glamour Girls; Bedding Down;* and the nonfiction collections *Best Sex Writing 2008* and *2009.* Her work has been published in more than one hundred anthologies, including *Best American Erotica 2004* and *2006,* Zane's *Chocolate Flava 2* and *Purple Panties, Everything You Know About Sex Is Wrong, Single State of the Union,* and *Desire: Women Write About Wanting.* She serves as senior editor at *Penthouse Variations,* and wrote the popular "Lusty Lady" column for the *Village Voice.*

Rachel has written for *AVN, Bust, Cosmopolitan, Curve,* Fresh Yarn, Gothamist, Huffington Post, Mediabistro, *Newsday,*

New York Post, Penthouse, Playgirl, Radar, San Francisco Chronicle, Time Out New York, and *Zink*, among others. She has been quoted in the *New York Times, USA Today, Maxim UK, Glamour UK, GQ Italy, National Post* (Canada), *Wysokie Obcasy (Poland), Seattle Weekly*, and other publications, and has appeared on "The Martha Stewart Show," "The Berman and Berman Show," NY1, and Showtime's "Family Business." She has hosted In the Flesh Erotic Reading Series since October 2005, about which the *New York Times*'s UrbanEye newsletter said she "welcomes eroticism of all stripes, spots, and textures." She blogs at lustylady.blogspot.com and cupcakestakethecake. blogspot.com.

To find out about the latest in hotel sex, read news about the authors, and share your own stories, visit the official *Do Not Disturb* blog at http://donotdisturbbook.wordpress.com.